G.U.N.

GROWING UP NUCLEAR

G.U.N.

GROWING UP NUCLEAR

FIL PIERCE

Columbus, Ohio

This book is a narrative memoir. It reflects the author's present recollections of experiences over time to the best of the author's ability. Some names have been changed to protect their privacy.

G. U. N. (Growing Up Nuclear)

Published by Gatekeeper Press
2167 Stringtown Rd, Suite 109
Columbus, OH 43123-2989
www.GatekeeperPress.com

The editorial work and typesetting for this book are entirely the product of the author. Gatekeeper Press did not participate in and is not responsible for any aspect of these elements.

ISBN (paperback): 9781662909481

Table of Contents

FOREWORD

With the growing, desperate need for everyone to start waking up to personal realizations about an atomic holocaust (despite governments wanting people to go to sleep), " Growing Up Nuclear" has found its era. The stories are based on the edited journals of Will Tully, representative of a generation born and raised during 70 plus years of interminable wars since W W II. The stories and novella chronicle years of frustration over a lifetime filled with, as Will states it : " wars and rumors of wars.; peace makes lousy rumors; no one believes them."

Will also describes the central enigma of his existence as: "I'm always trying not to think about the unthinkable. But if it's the unthinkable, how come I spend so much time thinking about 'The Bomb' ? " Throughout the journals, Fil Tully, Will's younger brother, emerges as the "editor " who provides introductions, transitions, and semi- objective interpretations of Will's often times arcane humor.

He also occasionally editorializes on Will's plight : " Will served in the peacetime Army. But he depicts himself as another kind of veteran: he's one of the walking - wounded of the global Nuclear threat; it's the longest list of casualties America ever sustained."

For Will, it started during W W I I. As he says, " After the war, my daddy just marched home one day, a total stranger unto me." Will admits the Bomb may have had a positive effect—like stopping WW I I—but it also began a silent reign of terror called " the Cold War ." Every man, woman, and child on the planet began facing instant vaporization.

At times, Fil gets in a lick or two re : "Congress is full of dead people who don't have the good sense to lie down; I'll stab your back if you'll stab mine."

Their shared experience of crisis and revelation, in the final novella section titled "Dogtags," brings a flash of light—that reveals the " hand-writing on the wall." Will, as an anti-war- anti-nuke protester, and Fil , as a defector from the Vietnam War, finally discover the nucleus of their lives.

Interspersed, occasionally, is a thing Fil introduces as: "Nuclear University Comparative Literary Evaluation And Review—NUCLEAR. " It's a revision of some classical poems as a gentle dig at Will's almost maniacal fixation with The Bomb. It will speak for itself.

"Growing Up Nuclear" tries not to be a mere " 60's as seen from the barricades " screed, or a simple, rabid " Ban the Bomb " tract. The whole work chews on critical questions that still need to be digested, such as: " Are we resigned, forever, to the global nuclear hostage syndrome? " It also seeks to reveal questions still un- asked, like: " Why are we still in Vietnam ? (it became spelled Afghanistan-who's next?) " Above all, the work takes the reader into the hearts and minds of people becoming adults during the epoch that hasn't ended with the Bang, or with the Whimper, or the first American president forced to resign. Whither now? In 1942, physicist Enrico Fermi commented on the first nuclear chain reaction experimentally started : he said the chain reaction has begun. Will Tully's reaction is "great, now when in the hell does it end? "

NOTICE: YOU CAN'T READ ON UNTIL YOU READ THIS ! !

I have a lot of people to acknowledge; and I know it's usually done at the end. But I am sure it will only be read if I put it up front. And I will start with the ones that go back the furthest with me :

My parents, Wilbur and Doris Pierce: We had our moments—great and not so great—but they stuck with me. And they tried to guide me towards the best path; and despite me, we all came out on the great side. And you gave me brother Tom, and sisters Deb and Shara. – and she gave me Niki-- I'll always love you all !

My children: Sean, Larisa, Erin and Cody—and grandchildren : Nik, Anikka, Sage, Allie, Olivia, Aiden, Sophia, Jerimia, Cadence, and Liam. I am so proud of all of you. And I will always be your Papa, and always love you.

Willy Stark –Wendy Davis: As of 2022, Willy and I go back to 1948, 72 years. I think I hear him saying, " it seems longer." We had many fantastic adventures including avoiding school, skiing, camping, scuba diving, and mountain climbing-- but the biggest was going to Alaska. We worked on the Alaska Railroad putting it back together after the big 1964 earthquake. And we also went homesteading in the wilderness-- one of the high points of my life. Over 60 years later, the cabin is still there, and we still hike up to it, me at 80. He is a highly artistic sail boat maker, and a mystic, and one reason I am sober. Also. I was a sort-of adopted son by his Mom and Dad, Bill and Peg Stark. Thank you my brother, love you, Tully.

Sherry Halbert-Pierce: We met about 1955, and became childhood sweethearts. We were married from 1962 to 1964; then she felt it wasn't working and she left. I went to Alaska, and then 51 years later I got a phone call. This woman started talking, and I said who is this? She said this is Sherry Halbert, and I said I think I need to sit down: we had not known of, seen or talked to each other, in 51 years. In 2015 we were remarried, and looking forward to the next 50 years to catch up; people live to be 135, right? I loved you then—I love you now and forever—You showed me what God can do for us-- thank you God !

Sandy Christen: after over 60 years, she still admits I'm her cousin. We grew up together around Grammy Ackley's family farm; and it was a magical experience. She went to Alaska, and married Willy ; and they went homesteading with the rest of us. She is still on the homestead 47 years later. Love you Cuz, and keep on keeping on.

Thor and Nancy Brandt-erichsen: These folks are real Alaskans. When I first went to Alaska, they took me in like a brother. We all went on the great adventure homesteading together. Thor was a genius, printer, artist, and cabin builder. On the homestead, Nancy took care of a one-year-old and a three-year-old, cooked for a crew, washed dishes, did laundry, and helped on the cabin. She taught school for over 25 years; and she has become a wonderful artist. And she has been a great friend for over 50 years ! Love,Tully

Kim and Ella Esterberg: we were in college together during the 60s, and you have been great friends ever since. You have always welcomed me in, and treated me like a brother. We have done so many wonderful things together, like sailing on your boat. And one of the greatest was hiking up to the homestead cabin. You have that sign that says: "friends are the family you choose for yourself." And you have lived by that. Love Tully

Bruce and Connie Marvin: Bruce and I taught public school at Trapper Creek, Alaska (population about 14 ½ people). We had some fun times, and weird times (do you know Manuel?) (Re a parent : "I want my kid to be a rugged individualist, so you let him do what he wants ; but I want him to be civilized, so you make sure he minds you while he's doing it " ??) And we had some fantastic travels in their RV over 15 years. We have walked a path, both physically and spiritually, and he helped bring me back to the Lord. You are great people and wonderful friends. Love you, Tully

Jim and Bea Hitchcock: Great friends, Great People, Great Alaskans. They took me into their home, like I was a brother, when I was at my lowest. Whenever I come to their house I say " Mom, Dad I'm home." We did so many fun plays together with Bea as the beautiful soloist ! Jim is the Renaissance man-- too many talents to name. But he is a genius log home builder. He is also a pilot extraordinaire : I was a documentary filmmaker for 35 years in Alaska. Jim and I made the first documentary of flying a private plane from the lower 48 to Alaska. It's called " Wings To Alaska." He has starred in many of my Doc's. I rode motorcycle for 50 years in Alaska. I made the 1st doc of riding to the Arctic Ocean. 500 more miles and I would have been at the

North Pole; but you can't ride a motorcycle on the ice pack. J-B, I love you and Lizard as my other magical family--Fil

To all my other relatives and friends: Big D-Sal, Dwayne, Grace-Mac, Ruth-Dave, EP-Bill, Karl, Jake-Jean, Riian-Loren-Dugan, Tim-Sharon : You have added to my life in so many wonderful ways—Thank you for putting up with me—Love—Tully-Fil.

"We don't need the Atomic Bomb
anymore; we have the Internet."

Bruce (check the breakers) Marvin

WORLD WAR II SEATTLE SUBWAY

Dedicated with love to my father, Wilbur Pierce, who
never brought home a subway.

Thanks Pops

A man in Seattle has a secret subway beneath his family home. He keeps it a secret, because the city of Seattle doesn't have subways; and he doesn't want to share it. He " liberated " his prize in Germany, 1945. Entering Berlin with the Allies, he was ordered to secure the subway. But, once taken, no one told him what to do with it.

So, he got a couple of buddies in the Corp of Engineers to crate up some of the tracks, an engine, and a couple of cars. Then he slipped a Liberty Ship captain a case of French Cognac to load it on board. His brother made a deal with some stevedores in Seattle – and there it was. " It's sort of a Lend – Lease plan in reverse," he explained to his brother who considered it the champion of all war souvenirs.

He spent the next four years, nights and weekends, creating a circular tunnel deep under his property. His brother had kept the family business going during the conflict knowing that construction outfits always do a thriving business after a war. Naturally, this was a perfect arrangement for our man's obsessive hobby, what with the hoisting cranes, and digging machines and all.

He had his wife sprinkle the soil on their food; "everyone has to eat a little dirt in this life," he assured her. Eventually his childrens' systems adjusted to it. They came to thrive on it, just like his war stories, which he told anyone who would listen. Five years later, he threw the final switch – and Seattle had a secret subway.

"This is what I fought the war for; this is what retirement is all about," he declares to his wife. Late at night, after dinner, and a bit too much bourbon, he strolls down to the basement and dons his old uniform (altered like himself by age.) Descending by a secret stairway, through odors of decaying earth and rusting metals, our man mounts his iron charger.

The setting is subterranean Berlin, 1945. " Kilroy Was Here" is even chalked on the tunnel wall. Around and around go the caravan of cars. Standing at the motor man's position, with coaches rumbling and flags flying, the Liberator salutes to prerecorded, cheering crowds.

"There's no problem," he informs his wife;   "we can take it off the taxes. I've listed it as a fallout shelter."

With kudos to R.B.

HIROSHIMA, MON TUTOR

Peering out through densely laden apple bows, gently, gently I pushed aside clumps of fuzzy, green fruit and scanned the hazy stubble field. Dusty heat waves rose over scattered, yellow straw chaff. Then, from the pigpen, silent, crouching figures cautiously filed out and crept across the mown July meadow. Fruit flies droned like a death in my ear. On the limb below me, my squad leader, Teddy, quietly released the safety catch on his rifle. " Where are they now, Will, " he whispered -- " say when! "

I clutched my green "hand grenade," and nervously bit into it again. Suddenly, a cold fist gripped my guts – this was it – the green apple shits ! My cousin Bob, the Nazi leader, silently led his storm troopers across the blazing stubble. Glancing furtively this way and that, they moved through our minefield. Here, finally, was my chance to purge the world of this scum. I prayed for them to come into grenade range soon, or they would not be the only ones purged.

Cousin Teddy nervously plucked three more " grenades." I wondered if he had discovered the high potency of these missiles, and was also experiencing a battle of the bowels. A Friday in 1948 was a green letter day in my life: I had met the enemy and it was inside me, screaming to get out. I concentrated on the outward enemy –Jerries, Nazis!

A short distance now, the leader of this Kraut patrol froze into a crouch and threw up a rigid arm. His men dropped to one knee and aimed their rifles in all directions. My God they were well trained 7, 8 and 9 year-olds. Such discipline – – Bob had thrashed me more than once for disobeying orders. Finally, in disgust, he refused to have me in the ranks. I was transferred to the other side; I was happy, and cousin Teddy was happy. He didn't give a shit what you did, just as long as he could be leader.

Now, finally, victory was in our grasp. The forces of rigid order and tyranny were about to be crushed by the spirit of freedom. We had multitudes of apples, and they had mere cap guns and a few windfalls. My guts roiled. Unable to wait for me to announce the whites of their eyes, Teddy lobbed a trajectory grenade into the center of the Nazi tableau.

Instantly the air was filled with hard, green projectiles, some whole, some with teeth marks, others half eaten. The trees swayed to the shouts of cousins and brothers, of all sizes, hurling things at each other. My brother, Fil, tried to throw them back; but it was too much firepower for a five-year-old. I had been assigned to an "observation post " on the highest, thinnest branch. In the heat of battle, I fell victim to my own intestines: a massive diarrhea cramp caught me in mid throw, and I clutched my belly.

"I'm hit! I'm hit! " I had seen the fall – from – the – tree scene at almost every W W I I Saturday Matinee. My plan had been to execute a short, but dramatic, drop to the next lower limb; there I would hang and deliver a farewell speech to my buddies. Then, hand over hand down the tree limbs, with the final sprint for the outhouse being my victory lap ; that was my plan. As usual, I didn't check with headquarters before introducing new strategy. Teddy, therefore, had no idea of clearing my flight path. Single-handedly, I destroyed my own command post, and delivered my squad leader into the hands of the enemy. We fell intertwined, shrieking and cursing to the earth.

I had no firsthand knowledge of the battle's outcome. In our frenzied drop, I wound up under Teddy, breaking his fall. Directly under that tree, a large rock broke my fall, headfirst.

A dazzling array of star shells went off in my head – – then darkness.

Years later, Kirk, another cousin, gave me his version of the scene: " Bob and Teddy called a truce to evacuate the wounded. Sam and Kirk hauled you across the cow pasture, blood gushing from this god- awful crack in your skull; all of us were scared shitless. Except you, boy did you stink! " In my baptism of fire, my bowels had betrayed me. I was, undoubtedly, the vilest P. O. W. ever to fall into enemy hands.

According to Kirk, Teddy performed an act of heroism that has forever endeared him to me. re Kirk: " Teddy danced around and around the stretcher bearers, waving his arms and chanting in a cracked, terrified voice: ' Fil ain't got no brother! Fil ain't got no brother! ' "

They handed me under the electric fence to my semi-hysterical mother, and uncle Babe, who rushed me to the nearest field hospital open at that time – – a veterinarian. The odor of medicinal alcohol , forever intermingled with the stench of shit, the feel of sutures, and black terror, are indelible memories.

I returned home less than a hero among the adults. The front room of my grandmother's house was filled with relatives, anxious to see my battle scars, and waiting to chew me out for a long list of sins. My mother wept for my injury – – wept for my recovery – – and wept for my stupidity. " Grammy " added one more tenant to the Geneva Accords: no more ambushes from trees ! The troops, however, were elated; I was the first real casualty.

The war went on without me. I convalesced and watched whenever any action was staged outside my window. Sitting up, and drawing Grammy's patchwork quilt under my chin, I gingerly turned my head against the big, soft pillows and watched the war; occasionally, scouts from both sides brought me reports of distant victories or defeats. After one particularly victorious Sunday, Teddy, my old squad leader, filed a report while I sipped an Orange Crush. He and rob had called a cease-fire to attend a war movie the day before.

"You should see the Princess Theater, Will. They have sandbags piled around the ticket booth, just like a real machine-gun pillbox; the girl was wearing a real G.I. steel helmet." He continued with a description of the movie "Battleground." After a blow – by – blow account of the film, Teddy proceeded to recount the present day's war games on the home front. He mapped out the battlefield on my color book with my crayons. Then, using my quilt as the terrain, he stuffed a pillow under the covers to represent the hill his troops had occupied.

Next, he began a detailed reenactment of the campaign, replete with crayons used to represent soldiers. Each time someone was hit, a crayon would hurtle down the slope, accompanied by explosive sounds effects and screams. " You should've seen it Will! Every time those guys would start up the hill, we would mow'em down with mud balls! It was a massacre!" Obviously, all of Saturday's maneuvers, thanks to Hollywood, followed the plot of the Matinee. Teddy became so involved in his narrative, he suddenly tried one of Van Johnson's lines on me. Producing a " Purple Heart" made of construction paper, he said: " what are you going to do after this war Will? "

I had been fighting this war for so many summers, weekends, and after school nights, I didn't have an answer for him. Anyway, his words didn't have any real meaning for me; our war had become just a game since my fall. But, I had earned that paper medal with a real battle scar, and real head bandages.

Teddy held out the award, and concluded with his usual finesse: "boy, you look like they dropped the A Bomb on you! Hey, in the newsreel they showed where we hit the Japs,

Hirmosha, or someplace . What a blast. You should have seen it, Will ! " Just thinking of it almost made me glad I couldn't go. I had somehow lost my taste for the mayhem of even play war.

After Teddy left, I got out my shoe box of special things: the newspaper article about Grammy wiring B – 29s at Boeings when I was four. My birthday card, when I was also four, greeted me with its foreign language and strange people, dressed in odd clothes. At the bottom, in a written hand it said " To My Son Will, from Daddy, somewhere in Germany, 1944. " It was a treasured keepsake from the real war.

As I clutched the card, a nearly forgotten feeling of dread settled over me. I sensed many long evenings being rocked to sleep in my mother's tense, clutching arms. Suddenly, I heard my mother's nearly sobbing voice reading aloud a series of letters. One reoccurring word was probably all I recognized at the time, the word "Daddy."

When the birthday card was first read to me, I didn't really know what a daddy was. Then, one day, a soldier came to Grammy's house, and my mother said he was my daddy, home from the war. I had learned about war, but not about daddy.

Now, I gazed at my card, while gingerly feeling my fresh battle wound. Instantly, the intense pain and awful blackness somehow related to another word I recalled from those war years. A fearful phantom had whispered that same word to me while my mother lay cradling me, sleeping. It also reoccurred as I lay on the operating table. I did not want to pronounce it then, or even now, even in my thoughts. But Death prevailed, as it always does. Tingling in my belly, I folded the paper medal, placed everything back in the box, and slowly closed the lid.

Big pillows stuffed behind me felt good on my head; lazy summer sunlight flowed across Grammy's hand – made patchwork quilt. Through drowsy lids, I read a message Teddy had doodled on my Real War coloring book. Red crayon boldly announced, "KILROY WAS HERE."

The war dragged on throughout that long summer and into the next decade. In June 1951, we finally introduced the ultimate weapon into the fray. But Nick, a new kid, tutored us in the awesome knowledge of what kind of bomb we were toying with.

Teddy and I once more found ourselves facing overwhelming odds. Sweating from heaving dirt clods all morning, we gazed out on a seemingly peaceful, fir forest, while munching on our acidic rations of Oregon Grape berries. "I think they went to the creek to get more water, Will. We're damn near out, but we don't dare try to get more." Teddy gave me a worried glance.

"Maybe they went home to lunch, and didn't tell us; " I probably sounded both hopeful and fearful. I didn't really want to face the final battle, especially on an empty stomach. A battle cry from the surrounding trees announced the inevitable. If an assault wave hit us, I knew we couldn't hold the line. The combined forces of Tojo and Hitler, in the form of many cousins including Bob, Kirk and the new kid Nick, closed in on our Fort of logs and sandbags. Green heat seem to rise with the dust of an advancing enemy in the deep fern forest of Pacific Washington.

Suddenly, I realized that " The Bomb " was our only hope; I'd read about it, but didn't really understand. I just knew it had ended the War in the Pacific, and now, in the 50s, it was even more powerful. Mud balls rained down on us, to the whistling and explosion sounds coming from the mouths of the enemy. I called to Teddy, " help me with this; it's our only hope."

Using the last of our water, we began rolling a mammoth mud ball. When it reached the size of a large watermelon, we gingerly lifted it up to a niche near the top of our fortress wall.

It's huge slickness felt cool and lethal. " Let's play dead, and wait until one of them tries to climb up," Teddy whispered. A quietness, as in the W W II jungle movies, settled over the dense near – tropical foliage. Below us, the ferns occasionally moved, as Bob's forces edged closer, fern fronds stuck in headbands the way we had seen the guys in the Pacific use them for camouflage. I crouched in front of a peep hole, and felt the mounting power in our muddy, cold super weapon.

Suddenly, a Banzi charge burst from the green shadows in front of us. Screaming, fern festooned troops poured out of the trees, and lunged for the log walls. Kirk led the pack, clambering up the logs and sandbags revetment, unknowingly dooming himself and his fellow warriors. I felt Teddy begin to rise; shoving the mud bomb up over the top log, we unleashed our last, desperate bid for victory.

The terror on Kirk's face was replaced with black, sloppy dirt, as he plunged backward, his screams mingled with our attempts at producing the final word in bomb explosion sound effects. Bob's troops stood stunned; they gazed in horror at Kirk, writhing in furious ,splattered anger. " You're all dead, blown to smithereens ! " Teddy shouted triumphantly. " Just like Hirmosha! " I added, gloating in my glee that we had been the first to use this marvelous new weapon that did the job with one big bang.

Our victory balloon was shot down, as rapidly as it had risen, with one deadly accurate outburst from Nick. " You're dead too! You're dead too! You can't use that thing without an airplane. It's not like a hand grenade, dammit! You can't get far enough away on foot in time; it gets you too ! " We weren't sure if he was right, but still felt victorious. Slowly, we helped Kirk up, wiped away the drying dirt caked on his face, and started home on the tree root tangled trails.

Discussing the day's discovery, we began forming tentative rules for the new warfare. " Let's say you can't use the Bomb on one person; you have to throw it on the ground next to the whole group, " Kirk implored. " Let's say you can only use Atomic Bombs if you run out of every other way to win, even if it gets you." Bob said in his usual, reasonable manner.

ANNOUNCEMENT FROM NUCLEAR UNIVERSITY

July 4, 2100 A B (After Bombs)

Enclosed is NUCLEAR: Nuclear University Comparative Literary Evaluation And Review

Scientists speculate that the radiation storms were so severe, they caused molecular distortion in everything, including the print in books. The original works were all classics of literature. How many of the authors and titles – – chapter and verse – – can you identify? The answers are not in the back. After reading a few of these, you will undoubtedly grasp the significance of the title of the text they came from: " Mutations."

As you read along in the book, " Growing Up Nuclear," you will encounter these distorted classics. Sometimes they relate to the story just after them. Other times the author is just showing off his Master's in Literature degree. But, obviously, they all relate to the subject of the entire work: the nuclear threat that is still creating, in a real sense, a Cold War that has congealed into a global glacier of fear, dread, and anomie.

In the spirit of Swift, I modestly propose that you study this sample of dark parodies. For the non– literary majors, there are obvious contemporary puns, jokes, and black humor injected into the old context. For all, there is a call for human reason and compassion to make itself heard over the dry, deathly rattle of plowshares being beaten into swords. I have provided the introduction. I feel that if we are going to write post – WW III parodies, we better start now. Read at your own risk.

Nuclear University Comparative Literary Evaluation and Review

By T.S. Electron

Last Of The Red-Hot Waste Lands

    April is the cruelest month, breeding

    Mutant Violets out of the lethal landscape, mixing

    Isotopes and genes, stirring

    Strange roots with acid rain.

    What are the claws that clutch, what grotesque branches grow

    Out of this nightmare rubble?

    And the blasted tree gives no shelter, the

    Blackened cricket no creak,

    And the melted, green glass no sound of life. Only

    There is shadow under this glowing rock.

    (Come in under the shadow of this glowing rock,

    And cool both heads.)

    And I will show you fear in a handful of atoms !

CHARLIE MCCARTHY MEETS THE WASTELAND

Under gray, gathering clouds, we fought our way up the ridge. Me ahead, Fil right behind, each wanting to be the first to see him. We had told everyone at school, "our cousin is home from Korea; he was at the real war, and now he's at our house !" The gravel road seemed endless, as we battled upward, straining, panting. Suddenly it was Pork Chop Hill, and I was John Wayne, pushing our men up and over the next ridge.   " Send 'em back to Tokyo," I shouted, hopelessly confusing wars and warriors.

Bursting through the door, in a human assault wave, I suddenly remembered the solemnity of the occasion: We were about to meet a real hero. It was a little disappointing, not finding Audie Murphy, medals cascading down his chest, swaggering through the living room. Instead, a tall, gangly, crew cut guy sat sipping coffee and talking quietly with my mother. She called him Sam, short for Samson.

Sam had landed the night before, infiltrating while Fil and I slept. He wore glasses and smoked Kools, but he had real dogtags under his shirt; I saw the chain around his neck. He had really been to the war! Fil and I shook hands with our cousin – hero, then made peanut butter sandwiches. Even with milk, it was tough to swallow and keep the stuff from sticking in our throats.

I wanted to start asking questions, but knew that if you asked a grown – up a direct question, they told you everything but what you really wanted to hear. Even if he was a cousin, Sam might start talking about Korea like Mrs. Rong did for

Geography class. We had studied about Asia, with boring lectures on the evil conditions that existed on that mythical continent. We heard how Chinese Communists (whatever they were) had invaded the tiny country of Korea, and how President Truman had refused to let it happen.

It all seemed so remote – not something you could get your heart into, like Nazis or Japs – it wasn't even a war ; they told us in school it was a "police action" (whatever that was). We all noticed, however, that G I Joe had been reassigned to Korea in the comics; after all, Japan had surrendered to him. And why had he returned to Asia, like MacArthur, if not to secure another victory for Uncle Sam? So, after school and on weekends we called it a war.

My cousin Teddy had his own formula for winning: "to heck with G I Joe; if we drop the A Bomb on them Koreans, they'd quit like the Japs."   We sensed that ducking and hiding under our desks had something to with A Bombs, and Russians, and surviving, but not sure from what. Much to Teddy's disgust, we finally outlawed A Bombs in our weekend wars – it ended things too quickly, with no winners. Also, Teddy was becoming trigger-happy with the things;   for him, surviving became secondary to winning.

But our cousin Sam had survived the real war, and returned a hero, like our G I's always did. We listen silently to mother and Sam, waiting for a hint of the terrible ordeal he had endured. By 6 o'clock, I was beginning to doubt the authenticity of this war hero cousin. He went on and on about whole regiments of relatives from North Dakota: who had married who; who had been born; who had died; (some ordeal).

"Mr. Chairman, Mr. Chairman, Mr. Chairman, I have in my hand a list of 200 card-carrying Communists in this administration….." " Senator McCarthy do you have any solid evidence for your accusations? " The TV started cutting into my concentration. Surrendering before me, Fil had retreated to the front room. I suddenly recalled bits of conversation about McCarthy appearing on television. I loved Charlie McCarthy on radio; I'd even seen him in newsreels of Bob Hope U. S. O. shows during the war. I raced into the living room hoping for an appearance by Mortimer Snerd – Charlie McCarthy was on TV!

"Point of Order – – Point of Order – – Point of Order…!" Some guy chanted this over and over. Another guy, who looked like he'd escaped from Dragnet, was sneering into the microphone: " and this traitor Rosenberg has given the Russians the A Bomb, and we're going to be living in fear for the rest of our lives… " In the audience, a bunch of people were going wild; others shouted out cries of "traitor, traitor! " Again the creep, " But the bleeding hearts in this country will excuse this left-wing pinko, as always… ! "

It wasn't my idea of a comedy, then I discovered it was a film on the evening news. Grim faces flickered across the black and white screen. Fil had headed for the basement. I kept an optimistic ear on Sam, and a pessimistic eye on the TV. Mother moved about the kitchen, in her quiet way, preparing dinner while visiting with Sam. " Just listen to that stuff Doris; I don't know what's happening to the world: we helped the Russians beat Hitler; and now they are trying to stab us in the back. They were even helpin' the Chinese in this war! Course they're all Communists," Sam said disgustedly.

When they started talking politics, I knew the battle was lost. Then I heard Sam mention the words "duffel bags," and a mental picture of two midget, green forms, lying on the basement floor, leapt into my mind. I had spotted them on a morning reconnaissance, before school, thinking this must be war booty.

Passing through the Rec room, I paused in the dark and stared at familiar black and white forms flickering across a hanging sheet. " Russia Stops Hitler " flashed across the screen: W W II newsreels, made into 8 mm home movies , I'd seen 100 times, were my last line of entertainment.   " You want to see it backwards when it's over, Will? " Fil's voice came out of the dark. " O K, yell when you're ready; " I couldn't resist the reverse effect.

Before I left, the same Russian Cavalry, dressed in Great Coats and fur hats, galloped towards, charging tanks with Swastikas on them, to their certain doom. Tight, squinting faces appeared from ruined buildings; stooped women clutched ill clad babies; both chewed on their clenched hands. In the next scene, the same women waived menacing fists at lines of Nazi prisoners shuffling by in the snow, rags on their feet. One behind the other, hands on their heads, hundreds trudged towards the rising sun. Grimy children with dark eyes stared, unsmiling, into the camera.

The line of P O Ws stopped and faced the camera. Hands in the air, they stood and stamped their feet first one than the other , over and over, frost smoke drifting out of their weary mouths. Every time I viewed that scene, the same question jumped into my mind: who were these men; and what would happen to them?

"I like it better backwards, especially the way those explosions swallow themselves up, and the bombs come floating back up into those Russian bombers. It's really neat! " Fil cheered on the aerial views of bombing raids flickering by. Above the chattering projector, he made whistling – falling – exploding sound effects, like in the real movies.

German fighters appeared, to be instantly engaged by cover fighters. " There's that fighter with "Kilroy" painted on it; go get em' Kilroy! " After 100 times I was still cheering. The bombers continued to drop their gifts from above. " Hey, how come they didn't drop an A bomb on Hitler? " Fil queried. I shrugged, and left.

Like small, green mummies, the duffel bags lay beside Sam's bunk. These were honest to God " battle bags," surely containing war souvenirs, (like the old man's German Luger, seldom seen and never talked about). But these spoils of war were hot off the battlefield, maybe even a fleck of dried blood on one of them. My faith in Sampson was renewed – – he was a real war G. I.

Upstairs, the old man was stomping in the door, cursing the cold rain that had started up. Mother sounded mess – call; "Fil, you and Will come up and wash your hands ... " And dinner proceeded with Sam calling the same roster of kin – folk "back in Dakota." It drove me to a triple helping of everything. "Sorry I can't stay with you folks longer, but I got to get back to Dakota an help the folks." Sam leaned back in his chair.

Would he really leave us without a report? He was still under orders, but he could tell us – – we were family! My mashed potatoes got drier and drier. I resolved, come hell or high water, if he didn't offer to open the duffel bags, I would make a frontal assault. Later, Dad began stoking up the fireplace; he carried in sections of black, dripping fir, while cursing the cold, drizzling Autumns of northeastern Washington.

"Never had to put up with this sloppy stuff all winter back in Dakota, did we Sam? " " Nope, just snow up to your butt, wind that blows the cows over on their sides, and they freeze there at below zero, Wilbur. " Sam and dad both chuckled. " Yeah – – you forget about that stuff when you haven't been in it for a while," said the old man, as he touched off a mound of paper. Firelight danced over the duffel bags in the dark corner. (Had he left them out for a reason?)

I lingered around the bags, but mother enlisted me in a search for the fireplace popcorn popper. The old man brought out a bottle and poured two large drinks, while the wood smoldered. Once the white popcorn was mounded up in a bowl, with yellow stripes crisscrossing it, everyone sat back and filled the with munching.

Between mouthfuls, dad talked about " the city of Seattle running the whole damn state of Washington." There followed a discussion about living in the big city, versus the benefits of a rural, small town like Midway on the Columbia River, our town. The old man finally asked the question which eventually got the response Fil and I had prayed for all day: " you going back to the farm, Sam? "

My cousin's answer released a flood of experiences and recollections: He started with a recounting of the drudgery of farm life, and moved on to a lament on the evil times that had befallen the country. Finally, in a surprise move, he shifted to – – Fil and I both sat up and chewed faster – – the war!

Sam sipped his whiskey and stared into the fire. " I don't think it's like it was for you, in Europe, Wilbur. We were both in field artillery, but it's a funny kind of war – – hell they don't even call it a war. You know, we dragged those damn cannons over the rice patties, mud up to your butt, and up those damn frozen ridges. But, we'd just get set up an' whammo! Our boys would be com'n back down the ridge – – followed by a whole gook regiment that came out of nowhere – – so damn close we couldn't hardly even fire."

Firelight flickered off Sam's glasses as he threw back his head; ice cubes clinked as he finished his drink. " We' d bug-out and tear back down the grade and across those patties. Next day, H. Q. would call wantin' to know where the hell we were! Just another day in the R. O. K." He grinned, knowing that would tickle the old man's sense of military mis- coordination. "Republic Of Korea," dad added.

"That sounds familiar," dad spoke softly. " I know they say this war is nothing like we've ever fought. Helicopters dropping guys off in the middle of enemy territory – – hostile troops showing up where nobody figured on them. They say we weren't prepared for it – – but when have we ever been prepared? " Dad leaned forward, poked at the fire with a stick, and sat back and drank.

Then, on one of those rare occasions, he spoke about his war: " When I joined the Dakota National Guard in 39, I was in artillery, and they issued us riding putees and horse blankets, left over from W. W. I. That was at the same time Hitler was building high-tech warplanes. But I will say this: Roosevelt knew what was coming, and put us Reserves into the full-time Army, and started training us. If not for that, we would have been just cannon – fodder; and I think we did a fair job holding the line. It really surprised the Nazi military – –Hell, it surprised our military.

"But, I'm afraid the day is coming when we'll have to be prepared and stay that way. And Like the man says: a standing army will always be used by somebody, eventually… ." " Yeah, they threw us into Ko-rea   green too," Sam agreed.   " But, you know Wil, I think it's different; they sent you over to win that war. But, Truman fired MacArthur when he wanted to push the gooks back into China. Course we had a real edge when we had the only A Bomb. Now, Russia has the bomb and is backin' China, and Harry's actin' like he's scared of the Russians droppin' the bomb on us."

"That's what Rosenberg did to us, Sam. We really lost our shirt when Stalin got the bomb; " dad shook his head. " Hey, shirts reminds me; " Sam jumped up and dug into the bags. My imagination exploded as he held up two packages with Oriental markings. Handing one to the old man he said, " they' re pure silk; I picked them up in Yokuska." He held up his prize, a shirt with ornate green and blue dragons crawling across the collar and shoulders; silk scales glittered in the firelight. " That one's for you. They're small, because gooks are all built small, Japs, Chinese, Ko-reans, all the same." Dad tried on his shirt, while Sam revealed yet another wonder from the East. As he removed the lacquered, cylindrical, engraved case, I knew I was about to behold a ceremonial sword, captured from the now dead Korean officer. " Banzi ! " My ecstasy could not be restrained.

Sam stared at me through arched glasses, then continued: "These were starting to come around just before I left…" He unscrewed the base and removed three sections of tapered dowling. "I don't know that I'll use the thing that much, but it was a real bargain. " Fitting the large section to the medium piece, and the whole thing to the smallest section, produced a tapering lance about 6 feet long. " I don't play pool much, but I'll bet the guys down at Sitzer's bar haven't seen one of these yet," Sam smiled; I sighed.

After repacking his war souvenirs, Sam and the old man sat around the fire and talked more politics. I surrendered, and resigned myself to the fact that Sam was going to be as closed – mouth about this war, as Dad was about the last one. I dozed with their voices droning on about Atomic Bombs.

"I don't know what the hell we're doing over there, Wil. We pushed them back to the 38th parallel, and they won't let us finish the job. We kill them, and the North Koreans just get more supplies from China, and more troops , and keep on goin'. We can't win that way and it looks like they can't either. Why don't they tell Stalin that we are runnin' the gooks back to China? And if he does anything to stop us, we'll give em' all a taste of what the Japs got at Hiroshima."

The last words I heard were from Dad; " what if Stalin tries to give us a taste of the same? There may not be another war – – which would be good – – – because there may not be anybody, anywhere, to fight one —which I think would be bad. But, maybe we'll learn something from this war? "

Nuclear University Comparative Literary Evaluation and Review

By John Doome

No Man Is An Isotope

> We are all made of the same stuff,
>
> A part of the protoplasm, the cosmos.
>
> One man's irradiation disintegrates
>
> Us all. Send not to know on whom the
>
> Bomb falls,
>
> It falls on thee !

By John Meltdown

Paradise Scorched

> And as I fell into that Witchs' coven,
>
> A presence gathered before me
>
> On the luminous air;
>
> The figure of one who seemed half- baked in a microwave oven.
>
> It spoke, " not man, though
>
> Man I used to be.
>
> A professor, both my parents were academics too;
>
> I was a pedant, and cared not, for bird or tree.
>
> We came to Seattle, after the disintegration
>
> Of Cleveland. But you – – why did you come
>
> to this ghastly, potential site of incineration? "

IKE BITES THE ATTOMIC BULLET

June 20th, 1958 – – I saw my first real, California palm trees this morning. They looked somehow different from all the World War II movies, in the Pacific, of a thousand Saturday matinees. Stopping on a siding woke me up, even after playing poker far into the night. Freight cars rattled by the grimy glass, then a dingy caboose.

As it cleared my vision, I was suddenly aware of odd, stilt – like figures standing in the sunrise; weird, dark shapes hunched over, bathed in hazy, but intense red rays. The novelty of cactus, later, was somehow diminished by the stark memory of that desert dawning.

Next, they transferred us to the Oakland ferry. It sloshed under the Bay Bridge, bucking an incoming tide of garbage. As we docked at the magic city of San Francisco, I upchucked my railroad club car drinks, then boarded the Greyhound. As the Army added whole new vistas to my experience, by train, by boat, and by bus, it shunted me southward, ever southward, towards " Fort Ord By – the – sea."

Sgt. Lee had escorted us aboard the train, the ferry, the bus, and had helped everyone get settled. He was firm but fair about us sticking together. All the ribbons and medals on his uniform looked real snappy. Then the bus rolled through the palm- lined gates of Fort Ord: Sgt. First Class Lee, U. S. Army, barked – " all right shit-heads off the fuckin' bus! " Instantly I knew had made a mistake.

June 21st – – we arrived at a place called the " Reception Center " last night. Fed at five, rostered and tallied at seven, we bunked at eight. The L. A. " Bebop's " were howling about it in pidgin English: " hey you loco putos, it's only 8 o'clock at night! " Even at 17, I had the feeling I was going to be very old, two years from now.

June 22nd – -Next morning, I discovered the reason for the early sack time: reveille at 4:00 AM seemed funny in the movies; the humor drained out of it instantly in real life. Red stripes on the barber pole bore witness to their original meaning: 20 chairs, no waiting – – 20 recruits all but strapped in – – stopwatch set – – and 20 power clippers roared on at the sound of the bell. The first " barber " with a totally shorn sheep stopped the clock. " I hear they award the ears to the winner," a voice behind me whispered quietly, very quietly. The arena reeked of singed flesh and medicinal alcohol. Some Reception!

June 23rd – – we were transported to another area. Lines of O. D. animals shuffled into the trucks taking us to the "Processing Center". Boarding the "cattle trucks," (they really called them that) someone started mooing; and the rest of us picked it up while the cadre went wild. (Upton Sinclair, where are you now that we really need you?)

Processing Physicals: "bend over and spread your cheeks!" What a pretty sight for some poor M. D. 100 hairy ass holes staring at him, right after breakfast. " Turn your head and cough! " Elephantiasis of the balls – – that was my diagnosis of the recruit next to me – – the doc hefted them in his hand as if judging rubber grape fruit . He mumbled something to the major - domo with the clipboard who motioned to Sabu. The young pachyderm put on his clothes and shambled out; I know everyone was thinking the same as me – – " you lucky bastard."

June 25th – – " they won't be so damn nice to you people up on Boot Hill," the Processing cadre assured us. Nice: shots, forms, more forms, forms again; clothing by Omar the Tent Maker; " check the teeth before you buy; " V.D. Lectures, no smoking, no talking, no spitting, hurry up, wait, no loitering; step to the next line, hurry up, wait. 5 AM till 9 PM – – Real Nice! The next day we headed for " Boot Hill," very picturesque name. They were forming up the Basic Training Company; anything had to be better than being Received and Processed !

June 28th – – no time to write for the last four days; no time to think for the last four days; these people are fanatics. I'm already getting sucked into this discipline thing they have going. Our Senior Drill Instructor, Sgt. Lopez (dubbed – not to his face – " Smilin' Jack the Wet Back ") is leading field pack assembly drill. I'm cursing my pack for refusing to obey a direct order; the things are still being re – designed by the proverbial infinite monkeys in a room.

Suddenly the silence is deafening – – Behold! – – Everyone in the room is rigid. In my wrath, I didn't recognize the garbled order shouted out " Ten-Shun! " (Strange how that mispronunciation produces that very sensation – tension !) There in the dusty California heat stands Lieutenant – 2nd class – Moore. Black swagger stick, capped with an empty cartridge casing, in his black hand, he's staring at me with glittering black eyes. I develop instant rigor mortis (why such fear? He can't hit me, can he ?) " Live riflemen have fast reflexes, son; the other kind don't ! " His voice is soft, scaly sounding. " Yes Sir! Lieutenant Moore, Sir !! "

July 1st – – " you don't want to get the ' Third Eye ' men. You got to keep your head down, until you are ready to throw: up and look – down! Up and throw – down again! And don't stand up in the same place, twice. My buddy, he stood up to look and throw at the same time, he got the Third Eye! The big Eskimo points a stubby index finger between his dark, almond eyes and flashes a mouthful of immense, perfect teeth. Grin.

Hand grenades at 6 AM. They give us " blue dummies," to get used to hearing that "chink" of the little lever flying off; I still hear that sound in my sleep. When they put the real thing in my hand, time stops– the power to blow a human being into pieces in my grip: Up and look – down! Up and throw – down again! Whump !   I feel the reverberations – no sound like it before – no sound like it since ! The smell of death in the cordite.

Parting shot, " there's 50 feet of steel spring coiled into one of these little beauties. It's like a thousand cobras in your hand – – It'll jump out and bite your enemy in a thousand places if you just get it where it's supposed to go." The big Eskimo pulls the pin, rocks back, and lets fly to one of his assistants who grabs it, and holds the blue missile aloft. " But, it's no good men if you wind up with the Third Eye!" Grin

Death is vastly amusing to some of these folks; even their practical jokes have grim overtones. For instance, consider the " Atomic Bullet." A rifle range officer had us all sit in the stands to observe a new tactical weapon. I should have been alerted when we were allowed to smoke. I light up a Lucky Strike and watch the haze floating up in the twilight.

"Bring in the secret weapon squad! " A range crew carries in an M1 rifle with a special tripod mount, like a machine gun; they position and sight the outfit. " Bring in the special round!" A corporal carries in an ammo box painted with green and white stripes; " that's the colors for "Radioactive' Materials," I hear a loud whisper near me.

"You're right, young trooper, " the captain's voice comes out of the gloom. " What you are going to see here is the ultimate in rifle squad firepower; you may be the one in your company to control this fearsome death dealer." He steps to the side and shouts, " lock and load the Atomic Bullet! " I feel queasy, like being ordered to witness a firing squad. "We're so damn close !" Another shaky voice.

Meanwhile, the special rifle is readied. " Be prepared to look away! " the captain calls. " On target! " one of the crew announces. " Fire! " The M1 cracks, predictably. Instantly a blinding, yellowish – red flare erupts from an area about 200 yards down range. A detonation follows, but it lacks the intensity expected. However, a genuine , very impressive, mushroom cloud rises into the sunset. " What kind of nightmare shit is that? " Another voice quavers; a stampede is imminent.

Finally, the captain assures us there is no danger of radioactivity. " That explosion was just gasoline and TNT. It's a joke we pull on all recruits." His voice cackles. " But I wish our scientists could give us a real one of those beauties; it sure could shorten a war couldn't it ? " " Be the first on your block to be the last on your block," a voice behind me murmurs. I'm suddenly reminded of mud balls.

July 4 – – I report from somewhere deep inside a wall locker at Fort Ord. According to Webster, the 4th of July is: "A holiday set aside to celebrate American Independence etc…." Cruel – cruel jest. We are up and at em' at our usual 5:30 AM, but no real training today. The cadres are celebrating the emancipation-- (Ho ho). My opening line, " deep inside a wall locker," refers to having Duane, a good buddy, seal me inside mine. It's hard to write by flashlight, standing up; but it beats scrubbing urinals for the third time.

We are cleaning the barracks (Re- cleaning the barracks, after cleaning the barracks, just before cleaning the barracks, then cleaning the barracks again.) It's become a cloying routine: move everything to one end of the bay; scrape the old wax off;

apply wax and move everything to the other end of the bay and repeat; buff endlessly. Repaint the hall walls and stairs, and scrub the latrines, including the ceiling; we can do it in our sleep – some of us do.

I fall asleep, and the " Spirit of the Bayonet " scenario runs through my brain, again: heat comes at you like small knives on the drill ground. The metal grooves on 100 bayonet handles engage the steel locking studs on 100 M1 muzzles. The D. I. Poet, Sgt. York, describes it as the " intercourse of the rifle and the long spoon." He calls us out by twos; a man from another squad squares off with me. " What is the spirit of the bayonet!!! " York's maniacal scream causes a reflexive spring to attack position.

My bayonet, with the sheath on, points at the throat triangle of a faceless form. Sweat crawls down my back. " The spirit of the bayonet is to kill !! " 100 voices scream out in unison; it's enough to freeze the water on my skin. In the 100° sun, my helmet cooks my brains. The circling form before me tries a vertical butt stroke to my chin with his rifle – I block with port arms – the buckle on my sling catches me in the mouth – I taste blood ! I rush him – he's off balance and going over on his back... .

"To Kill ! To Kill ! To Kill ! " The chanting voices are suffocating, like the hot dust . I lunge forward, rifle aimed at his throat. Eyes wild, he flails at me with his useless weapon in one hand. Taste of blood – chanting – heat – " Oh Jesus ! " The sheath has dropped off my steel – it's naked and I can't stop – I'm falling on him...! " Tully, get your ass out of that wall locker; what the hell you doin' in there? " My squad leader saves me from a nightmare, only to return me to the real nightmare.

July 6 – – I'm back cleaning toilets, and hearing rumors of war. " Tully, you heard what's happenin' man? That asshole

Eisenhower – he's getting us into a war, someplace in Arabia! " Little Raymos, from L.A., is wide-eyed and breathing hard. " Shit, it ain't gonna' happen; they won't send green troops into a war-zone, would they? " Carson, the gorilla from Portland with a near- cracking voice, blurts out.

Mcnary, nicknamed Canary, the Jew from Sacramento, is driving everyone crazy. With his G I eyeglasses and G I haircut, he looks like an actor from a W W II Holocaust movie. " My mother will have a heart attack if they send me! My girl – were getting married – what'll I do Will? " " Canary, shut up! They're kidding, " a voice tries to convince itself. Canary : " Was Hitler kidding ? " (I swear to God, I'll send him to the showers.) " Canary, if you ask me what I'm going to do after this war, I'll kill you before they do ! " (Why did he pick me as a kindred soul?)

Maybe it's because I suffer also; but I suffer silently (perhaps too silently?) I'm trying not to hear Canary – I'm trying not to hear any of it. I'm concentrating on a bit of graffiti I saw etched on the shit-house wall at the rifle range: gazing at the ceiling only produced " Kilroy Was Here." Attempting to deaden the continual roar of musketry, I mentally repeat rhyme after cloying rhyme – " Here I sit, brokenhearted… ." Suddenly, I see this message scrawled in yellow, target – marker crayon: "I Don't Like Ike, Anymore !" And below it, in a larger, more defiant hand: " NEVER DID!!! "

The Drill Instructors are getting a big kick out of fanning the fires: as we are marching, they call out " Lebanon, Lebanon here we come!" And they repeat "Goin' down to Quartermasters to get our camel saddles, men ! "

July 16th – – crawling the " Infiltration Course" makes it all real. Sand grinding into my knees, elbows, and face, and the sound and smell of explosives all around. In Army patois: it wakes me the fuck up! This time it isn't from a nightmare; it's into THE NIGHTMARE! You can't see 50 caliber machine gun bullets searing the air 3 feet over your upturned face, not even the tracers at night. But you can hear them cut the air: wock-wock-wock ! (Don't stand up, men !!!) Dante would be right at home: Blackness, mud, and deathly greenish – white flares floating overhead; machine guns chanting in rhythmic cadence; TNT charges shaking the ground all around; and hanging in the air the smell of burning cordite – I am infiltrated by the feeling that it's a real war over there; and suddenly it's personal. I can faintly smell alcohol and the taste of green apples while death whickers over my head –WOCK! WOCK! WOCK!

August 8 – – Ike sent the Marines into Lebanon! For the first time in my life I have sort of an answer to that ageless question: after this war, I'm going to write a letter to Eisenhower, personally thanking him for rejecting my attempt to join the Marine Corp. If I don't win the Third Eye on the Infiltration Course, or get impaled on the Spirit of the Bayonet, I may even live through the Army. One year, nine months, and three days to go; actually, only three weeks of Fort Ord(deal).

But, the words "Basic Training" will always revive in me the sense of dread I experienced the last night. We were in the field on maneuvers, playing war, (like in the apple tree days.) I had perimeter guard duty, and they gave us blank ammunition to make it seem more real. I paced along in loose sand, threading my way through patches of ice plant, silently cursing my buddies who got to sleep.

My M1 hangs like an anvil on my shoulder. Our instructions were to keep the bullet clip in our pockets, but it makes a bulge that chafes my leg. So, I load the rifle, but keep the bolt open. Sleeping sounds float from black tent spaces.

"WHAT IS YOUR FIRST GENERAL ORDER!!!"

All of my childhood playing at war and Army combat training takes over – in one motion, the weapon comes off my arm sling - I slam the bolt home - and a blinding, yellow explosion kicks the steel rifle butt into my shoulder!!   " Son – Of – A– Bitch-Boy! you damn near blew my face off! " Lieut. Moore grabs the rifle from my frozen grip. His ghostly, black face emerges from the afterglow, as my night vision returns. My stomach coils up like the steel spring in a hand grenade.

"What the hell is going on? " Sgt. Lopez lopes toward us, his brown legs wrapped in khaki shorts, as revealed by a flashlight bobbing at his side. " Sgt. relieve this man of his weapon, and find someone to take his place on guard duty. " Moore remains firm, but a bit stretched. "Sir, what did he do?" Lopez sounds cagily curious. "He nearly killed me! I just stepped out to shake the dew off my lilly, and decided to test our perimeter defense." He sounds like a man telling "combat stories, " afraid someone might question him.

"Wouldn't you say that he passed the test, sir? " Lopez's smile flashes quickly in the dim light. Other forms begin to appear in the gloom; questions come from tired voices.   " Everyone go back to sleep! That's an order! " Lopez waves the flashlight beam like a sword. " Keep that clip in your pocket, like you were ordered to, Tully! Carry on, Sgt.! "   I salute mechanically as Moore fades into the shadowy tent yard.

"Not following orders kills more than it saves, Tully; that's why there's orders. But, those reflexes of yours will keep you a live rifleman, instead of the other kind. Carry on, young trooper." Lopez turns and saunters away.   As the darkness starts to wrap around me again, another vision forms in my brain: I see myself aiming a live rifle at a shout in the dark, and instinctively pulling the trigger. I don't fully realize it then, but for me the war is over.

Postscript: Stationed in Texas—Fort Bliss—what a misnomer. Crossing into Juarez, Mexico, I hate to say I became the hideous American. At 17, I attempted to drink Canada Dry, in Mexico! Unfortunately, not a joke . We did not have a drinking problem: we drank—we fell down—we gave the Mexicans shit – no problem. At least I did not avail myself of the senoritas of the salons.

Nuclear University Comparative Literary Evaluation and Review

By Oscar Wildeman

The Ballad of Radium Goal

This too I know – – and wise is it were
If each could know the same – –
That every bomb that men may build
Is built with shards of shame,
And bound with lies less Christ should see
How men their brothers maim.
The vilest deeds like poison weeds
Bloom in a nuclear pall.
And everything that's good in man
Should shriek and howl, and call,
" When you have seen one nuclear war
Buddy, you have seen them all ! "

Editor's Note: By Fil Tully

As Will himself put it, " after the Army, I was in and out: in and out of jobs, in and out of college, in out of love, and in and out of my mind! " He was a lifeguard, a printer's Devil, a live - in houseboy (at a sorority?) a longshoreman – " I drank my lunch wit' the best of em' on the docks of Seattle." –and a seller of " Praise Soap ? : No thank you young man-but do you praise the Lord ? " And he discovered what he dubbed as his calling: " I became a neo--quasi –' p'seudo (I pronounced the p)-- existential –retro philosopher : i.e. a professional student and Hippie ." When he ran out of money to go to school, he went back to work, shoving long hair up under his hard-hat.

But, going to work for Boeing Aircraft Company, in Seattle, was more than a job. According to Will it was: " an education in how the Defense Department spent more money than 10 generations could pay in taxes. And then they built ' Dooms – Day ' stuff that might negate those generations! (At least they wouldn't have to pay the taxes.) " He was hired into the Aero-Space-Division and discovered his new assignment: building ground support equipment for the Minute Man Missile System. He lasted six months.

For the rest of his life, he refused to talk about that experience. It was a sore place in his past; and if the subject of missiles came up, Will avoided it. In 1962, Will moved to the town of Moses Lake, Eastern Washington. He had courted and married his childhood sweetheart, Sherry, and after Boeing they needed work.

His next " theater of operations, " (pun mine) was manager of the Lake movie theater in Sherry's hometown of

Moses Lake. That fall, the Russians tried to sneak missiles into Cuba. To quote Will, " if Boeings was an education in real life, Atomic Al and the Cuban Catastrophe was an education in real death! "

The " Missiles of October, 1962 " however, were just a prelude to ghastlier realities. One year later, on " Black Thursday, 1963," John Kennedy's Cuban policy may have made " the chickens come home to roost; " (a quote by Malcom X, Black Panther .) Both dates are pivot points on which multitudes of minds turned toward a new phase of American political realities. The following entry is Will's fusing of two ultra - traumatic episodes that contributed to his becoming (again his own expression) "decontaminated."

JFK MEETS ATOMIC AL

Journal of (The Plague Years) November 22nd, 1963 – watching gray, cardboard figures flicker across the screen, I swallow another mouthful of stale, warm beer. I really can't feel much – I've turned off the sound – it's just re – runs of the same scene: a parade meanders down a dusty Dallas street; a car approaches and hands wave in front of the camera lens; two figures, a man and a woman, smile and wave from the limo convertible; the President passes.

Suddenly, people are running away from the scene, and the camera is struck and knocked around. Frantic forms leap out of focus as the cameraman falls. The final scene is being shot from ground level with the camera on its side. Down the street, the limo is stopped and men are frantically rushing for it; a woman is climbing out over the trunk. I drink mechanically. Fade out, and a photo of John Kennedy appears, with the visual readout of the latest details; the dead picture is smiling, and I'm crying for the live man. Drink – cry – drink.

I'm also recalling a live Kennedy, operating on the high wire, when "grace under pressure" meant no safety net for any of us: October 31st, 1962, a Halloween of real, not imaginary horrors. All the cold, long day, tense news bulletins came over the radio and TV – Grimm, grimmer, grimmest…

"Kennedy has given the Russians an ultimatum: no missiles in Cuba! He says he'll stop their missile transport ships in international waters, if they try to enter the Caribbean. The Russians are talking ' the ultimate retaliation. ' " Tight – lipped, cigarette shaking, our boss, Martin, delivered this cheerful bracer and headed out.

Shuck, and my wife Sherry and I managed the Lake theater, Saturday matinees and nights. For Halloween, Martin had booked in a sci-fi horror flick, " The Atomic Man," a bit of grotesque irony right out of Kafka. I eventually dubbed him Atomic Al, for the ordeal we subsequently shared on that All Hollows Eve. It made us comrades in catastrophe; our baptism of bombs began with the Saturday matinee.

It was a routine set up . After Martin's pepper – upper concerning the missile crisis, we vowed no Atomic Man for the kiddies. Walt Disney would hold sway this afternoon. Pete, the projectionist, came reeling in, breathing a blast of bourbon, prepared to " run the god -damn film backwards; give the little bastards a real treat! " I talked him out of it. " God -damn Cuban Castro, bearded banana beak," were Pete's parting words.

He groped his way up the stairs, appearing not to be in any worse shape than normal. But, as I was to find out, firsthand, the missile crisis was making bar owners rich beyond their wildest dreams. I was at the snack bar when the lights dimmed in the "snake pit." Closing the isle curtains, I glimpsed the beginning of previews. In the ticket booth, I grabbed a smoke while Shuck and Sherry pushed popcorn. I swear, if you lived in the damn place, you'd still notice that stale, greasy, succulent smell. I flipped on the radio – no news is bad news, if you don't listen – and quickly flipped it off.

My first hint of impending doom was an abnormal collection of smaller kids in the lobby. They usually waited for the first 15 to 20 minutes of the feature, before starting their unending migration for popcorn, then Coke, then water , then un-water. I drifted out to check on these early nomads : " what's up kids – Disney no good this time? – give it a chance guys." A wide-eyed urchin, clutching a sister and a box of Good and Plentys, stuttered : " no, it's, it's really nnnneat. But Sally can't watch what hhhhhappens to that guy when he turns into that radioactive tttthing – he looks like a burnt up marshmallow – Sally's scared but not me! "

Just then, a welter of screams poured up out of the aisles, followed by an exodus of hysterical children : small brothers dragging smaller sisters; older sisters pushing whimpering young brothers ahead of them; a herd of spooked calves stampeded out the front door. Shuck and Sherry tried to out- ride them. Chaos and terror rose from below, as I burst into the projection booth. Disney was still in the can – the Atomic Man writhed across the screen. A real trick - or - treat from Pete as he sprawled across his cot, out cold. I threw on the house lights.

At the front door, Sherry was handing out rain checks to irate parents. Shuck called Martin, and he had his answering machine on. We thanked God for our own machine; it rang like doom. " When these parents cool off, maybe they'll see it as sort of funny... " Shuck said hopefully.

That evening, Atomic Al, along with Pete, was revived; but the really big picture outside sailed on-and- on. The radioactive Russian ships were proceeding, despite the presence of P. T. 109. As an Air Force Cpl., from the nearby S. A. C. Base, Shuck assured me that the " Mon-row Doc-treen " would be our rod and staff; it failed to comfort me. Listening to Shuck expound the merits of Kennedy's position, while the Atomic Man mutated away, was like hearing a lecture on euthanasia, while watching a documentary on the Nazi death camps.

Being the only three viewers, Shuck, Sherry, and I shut the place down. Like moths, we were drawn to the irradiant glow of a television screen at the Turf bar. Apparently, after hearing reviews of the movie from their children, the rest of Midway drew the same parallels as I did. Hoping for the best, expecting the worst, we drank our way through a multitude of news flashes, and a myriad of political theories from the floor.

By midnight, the locals had a strategy for solving the crisis all mapped out. (I think I recall a resolution to call Kennedy, collect naturally.) Their re- assurances, that the "final solution" could never really happen to us, made me thirstier.

Outside, we wavered at the curb. I was waiting for the crisp October air to equalize with the whiskey fumes in my head. I was leaning against a building, in case it should falter in its stride. Shuck headed home, and Sherry and I were about to do the same. Suddenly, a rising growl became the moaning wail of a siren, echoing down the chilly, gritty streets. Icy air hit the bottom of my lungs, and frosted my entire system. It felt as if the building was falling on me.

"They've done it! Dammit! They've pushed the button! It's all over- those sons of bitches! " I started to run down the street, shouting at all of those smug storefronts – " it happened, it happened! And you told yourselves it couldn't! " And I suddenly knew how it felt not to have an older brother who could take my hand and lead me out of this horror movie. And then I heard somebody giggling.

I flipped around, and there was Sherry laughing her head off. I thought maybe it had all unhinged her, and I would have to deal with that. " Stop! Stop! We can't go off the deep end," I implored her. But, she looked at me and said, " that's the midnight fire siren test; they blow it once a month at midnight. Happy new year! " She grew up here; I'd been here less than a month. The siren wound down like a wounded animal accepting its pain. That was 62', and Sherry and I lasted until 64'. I don't blame her; she said it just wasn't working for her; we said our goodbyes, and she left .

What is left to say about November, 22, 1963 ? The shot reviled around the world; Kennedy's and a dream's demise. While I'm packing my bag on this cold, 1964 November night, I suddenly wonder if anyone ever asked JFK , " what you gonna ' do after World War II, Jack? " If he were clairvoyant, and really knew the full scenario, would he have come home? I come across an old playbill advertising, "The Atomic Man." I decide to leave it at Sherry's folks' place for her as a souvenir. But first I write across it in marker: " Kilroy is going to Alaska."

Fil's Fuge : with no offense meant to JFK, or the family.

"I'll always remember where I was the day it happened…." Naturally, everyone remembers where he or she was – but can they prove it ? My solution to the JFK murder is a bit complex, but no more unrealistic than what has been already proposed. It's a simple matter of accounting for everyone alive, in America, the day of November 22nd, 1963.

We have the technology: computers with AI; huge arrays forming clouds beyond tera - terabytes; voice and face recognition programs; and we could put the military on it. Beyond that, we could send in the real pros, who know exactly who everyone is, the IRS.

Essentially, all you have to do is prove that you were nowhere near Dallas on that date. But if you were in Dallas, you just need three witnesses to swear you were nowhere near the Texas Book Depository. It's a process of elimination . (A note from your mother will not suffice.)

I love the man as much as Will does. And we both hate that the American government had Spooks then, and a lot more Spooks now. And that all governments have Spooks, counter-Spooks, counter- counter- Spooks, and of course Nukes and Counter Nukes. Despite the Warren Report, there will never be actual justice for JFK. And how about actual justice for the American people?

Will followed Horace Greely's advice in his usual fashion: he went West to Seattle, but then went North to Alaska. As Will put it, " I had to go to Seattle and make a grub stake first. And like an addict, when I get money, instead of going to the Gulf of Mexico to write my novel, I enroll at some damn college.

"Then, I met some folks who had an intense curiosity about what the US government was up to. Before it was over, I'm positive the FBI rescinded my Top Secret Security Clearance from Boeing; and they undoubtedly shifted my file from the right-hand to the left-hand side of the playing board; and we met some Hoover salesmen with hard-sell tactics that took me back to the Army bayonet course; and when I woke up, over a year had gone by! " The reference to Hoover salesmen is the reason for the title of the next section.

THE HOOVERING : OR, TRIAL BY VACUUM

In full flight from the Cuban Missile Crisis of 1962, and JFK's murder of 1963, and the divorce of 1964, I landed in Seattle, in February, 1965, en- route to Alaska. Needing cheap housing, and traveling money, I gravitated toward the University of Washington District. Making a grub stake, and heading for the wilderness in May was my goal. Somebody said: " if you think you can tell the future, you'll find you can't tell it much." I said that.

Then I met this crazy guy called Joe who introduced me to some other people, like myself: i.e. Spooked of Nukes. They, however, were trying to do something constructive about it. I made a little effort, that's how I first met Joe's group at a Ban-the-Bomb rally. As the main speaker decried " the re- occurring ice age of international politics," a lady name Sheila ironically pointed out that " all the participants now have the means to instantly melt real glaciers." I agreed, and we started to talk.

Joe, Sheila, Roy and others were really into US foreign policy. They were just beginning to hear about Uncle Sam's involvement with a small South East Asian country called Vietnam. March 1965, Joe publicly revealed some sobering information: Ike, JFK, and LBJ between them, had rounded up a posse of 23,000 US " military advisors " (we called them " the Domino Theory Gang,") who had ridden West to head off the Commies at the Hiphong pass in Vietnam.

I was more on the fringe of things, looking over the landscape, a traveler passing through. For economy, I moved into a room at a place called "Cockroach Manor," a neo-commune shared by Joe, a Political Science major, Sheila, who dug history- philosophy, and others of similar commitments. All younger than me, but seriously dedicated to banning the Bomb and world peace.

I got a job as a Printer's Devil at a small job shop in Rainer Valley. The old man who owned it was the editor, staff, and management of the Italian language newspaper for the Rainer Valley. I didn't need to know the language for the stuff I did. I tried quizzing the guy about Garibaldi once; all he wanted to hear was Victor Emmanuelle. But we got along great, and ate pizza his wife made. No Pizza Pit for them. For a while I was also a live-in houseboy for a Sorority. But there were no benefits, so I returned to Joe's place.

Then, as the Seattle rain warmed up – a sign of Spring's arrival – Joe and crew began writing letters to the State Department , inquiring about such arcane subjects as: the 1963 Military Assistance Command established and still operating in South Vietnam; also, present US commitment to that country; and President Johnson's and Congress' views on all the above.

The Cockroach Manor crew became infamous by holding lectures at a room upstairs above the Pamir coffeehouse. Handbills subtly advertised the speeches as " Explorations of the Roots of World War III." But, interspersed with facts about the current crisis were stories about one man's anti-war story.

Gandhi's life and times were a reoccurring theme in the lifestyle of Cockroach Manor. (I now realize how accurately that small group pinpointed the coming problems, and some of the solutions) As if by some law of natural attraction, their curiosity about the government's activities aroused the government's curiosity about their activities. The 4th of July, 1965 remains in my mind, like a permanent after-glow from a sparkler.

I woke up, not knowing where I was, with firecrackers going off in my head. I focused on a gaunt specter in a ragged fatigue jacket, and a long blonde hair-beard combo, seated in a rocking chair. " Is it World War III out there yet? " I croaked. " Naw, it's neighbor kids blowing the mailbox off the front door. I'm Bill," he said and began a quiet rendition of "We Shall Overcome" on a battered guitar in his lap. " Who am I ? " I asked, eyes closed, brain off. " You're the guy who flagged me down on Brooklyn Avenue last night, and told me you were too drunk to walk; so you tried to commandeer my motorcycle. I told you that I had to do the driving, and you said ' you drive— I'll drink ' Then you tried to direct me to your place. But that didn't work, so we came to my place."

"… And we had a Independence Party. I recall someone reading the first lines of the Declaration of Independence " I said. Bill rejoined, " Yep, that's when you yelled, 'give me liberty or give me another beer! ' And you went down like a burnt rocket." He strummed the refrain from Dylan's " Blowin' In The Wind." " Was someone at the door, earlier—I heard voices— course I hear them all the time" I said.

Bill smiled, "nope, those were real. Damnedest thing I ever saw, man. This cat introduces himself as a vacuum cleaner salesman. Shows me some suitcases and starts into a demonstration, all the while asking about you, and a guy named Joe, and what kind of speeches were given at the party. Wants to know do I live at a place called Cockroach Manor, and how do I feel about our Foreign Policy. I never saw a salesman working on a big holiday. Real weird Daddio – I threw him out."

Bill's experience gave me an uneasy feeling. " Take me to Cockroach Manor on your murdercycle, and we'll ask Joe what he thinks of Hoover sellers on the 4th of July. " I rose, gingerly; outside, the hot air smelled of burning gunpowder. Joe, Sheila,

Roy and others all reported visits from " vacuum types " over the previous weeks. New faces – suit and tie variety – at the W W III lectures confirmed our suspicions.

"For those among us with everything to hide, we've prepared a little skit entitled: "What's My Real Line? " Joe and crew set up a few props and the weekly lecture became a political satire. " Our mystery guest is signing in. You say you employ vacuum salesmen, is that right Mr. Hoover ? The secret is panel, what are the Hawks really Hawking ? "

Joe came in with a dark suit, and a Bowler Derby. Roy, the moderator did a Groucho Marx move with his cigar and asked some random questions. Joe gave a few flaccid answers, then launched into an interrogation concerning the panel 's politics: "Are you now, have you ever been, or do you plan to throw a Communist Party? " Roy began chanting, " point of order, point of order, point of order… ." One panelist rose and yelled "cheeseburgers and Cokes for the house! "

Doing a waiter bit, Groucho wrote it on his tie with the cigar. Meanwhile, Joe whipped out a role of adding machine tape and, holding one end, spun it down the aisle: "Mr. Chairman, I have here a list of two and one- half Commies on this campus!" Roy rose and shouted, "I see your two and one- half, and raise you three and one-quarter." And then, Groucho leapt up and declared, "I can't see your three and one- quarter; can you bring it closer to me?" Another panelist yelled "this play will be immortal!" And Roy responded, "hey, you hear that – we're immoral; they need to vacuum us clean!" It brought down the house.

Unfortunately, the " immorality" play brought down the Morals Squad of the Seattle police on Cockroach Manor; even the building safety inspector got into the act. Within two weeks the building was condemned, and we all got eviction notices. By the third week the city literally brought down the house.

But then the US government dropped the Bomb; the radiation would engulf the entire country over the next 10 years. Joe broke the news: " After a multitude of the Vietnamese died throwing out the French colonials-- for about 100 years of guerrilla warfare-- that ass hole LBJ just announced: about two weeks ago he secretly sent the 1st Marine Division into South Vietnam.

"So the US had helped to partition Vietnam into two countries, like they did Korea; and the guy who runs North Vietnam, Ho Chi Mihn, is trying to reunite them. I talked about the 'military advisors' we have over there; well the Big Texan is sending full force troops to try and stop the re-unification. " Joe continued: " Remember we discussed that ' Domino Theory: ' the US is claiming the Communists are trying to take over all of Vietnam, and if they do, they say all Southeast Asian countries will fall like dominoes."

Sheila was the first to ask, " what does this mean for us, Joe? " He rep[lied : " Well, I had an idea it would come to this. It's one of the reasons we've been studying the guy in the turban and loincloth; we are going to have to go into High Gear Gandhi. If we go for violent protests, it will give them the excuse to go with violence. We need to take the playbook from the Civil Rights people. We are going to have to spread out, and spread the word as far as we can." We all looked at each other.

The sun was rising, along with the smell of a cool salt mist, and the Space Needle towered above us, while icy Mount Rainer floated in the distance. Joe, Sheila, Bill, Roy, and some others, stood at Pier 46 on Elliott Bay. " Where to now, Joe? " Roy asked, like he wasn't sure he wanted to hear the answer. But, Joe was still on top of it: " we'll all go our ways; but we'll see each other again. Just remember Gandhi's path: he fought the British to a standstill, economically, legally, and morally, and used the system against itself, to right a gross injustice. Like Jesus, he appealed to man's moral spirit: Render unto the IRS" he paused, " but don't get sucked into the vacuum ! "

We all had a good laugh. Bill hugged us all, climbed on his motorcycle, and roared away. " He's headed for California, going to school at Berkeley," Sheila said quietly. " He'll carry the message even though they seem to have part of it, already. Like you Roy, when you transfer to the Graduate School at Colorado." She smiled and glistened. One by one, saying adios, the others headed for the four compass points of the country, knowing what they were going to do.

"I guess you'll have to carry the news to the Eskimos, Will," Joe grinned. We all hugged and started our separate ways. Eventually, I realized why a handful of people, in a remote corner of the country, warranted such concentrated scrutiny by the mighty US government. Joe, and people like him, spread out over college campuses, workplaces, anywhere where they could get a toe hold, and began trying to organize.

California came up with "Flower Power." Eventually it came to a showdown, and you had that jaw-dropping photo of a war protester placing a flower down the barrel of a gun held by a soldier. But there were a lot of miles before that, and a lot of miles after that: 10 years – the longest war in US history, at that time.

I wandered down that Seattle dock, waiting to get on a fishing boat headed for Alaska. I was thinking I would fish and then, after the season, stay and see what kind of job I could get. I gazed out over the ocean, feeling like I had a good solid plan. Sometimes you think the future is something you can see; but sometimes the future is like the sea: the tide rolls in – the tide rolls out – and it's a whole new beach you've never seen before.

Editor's Note (Again!)

Will arrived in Alaska, and did okay fishing. And in November, he got on with the Alaska Railroad as a track- layer, also known as a Gandy- Dancer. His letters screamed about the beauty of the fantastic country, especially around Prince William Sound: " Fil, you should get your butt up here! I took a short flight in a light plane, and the animals, the forests, the lakes, the hills, the ocean, the mountains – it'll knock your eyes out! It's so damn vast, a man couldn't see it all in his lifetime! "

And sometimes he sounded like Jack London: " I'm on the Alaska Railroad as a section hand, laying ties and track. They go in for a direct form of justice here on the frontier. Clyde, the Bull-Cook, was a dead ringer for a cook I knew in the Army: his favorite expression was ' you can have your eggs any way you want , as long as it's scrambled.' And drunk, Clyde surpassed even himself in new levels of churlishness.

"I speak of him in the past tense, because the crew settled Clyde's hash browns last night. He came reeling in, his normal abrasive, wasted self, collapsing on a cot in total oblivion. When the night- shift brought a train engine up alongside the crew bunk- house, they left it running, like always. With groggy curiosity, I watched through the window as Curly, a bald guy from Seward, and Al, a trapper from Nome, carried Clyde out – and he was out – and laid him on the tracks in front of the engine.

"Then, Curly climbed up into the cab of the engine with its gleaming headlight, and languidly chugging diesel. The entire crew car went ape when Curly blew that damn engine horn, like dozing inside the lighthouse when the fog horn starts. But, the crews' reaction to being startled out of its sleep was nothing compared to Clyde's.

"I don't even like to imagine the sensation of being yanked out of an alcoholic stupor, and feeling cold iron rails reverberating to the rumble of a diesel engine, while a locomotive wails and casts its baleful, yellowish light upon me. In Clyde's state, I know he couldn't have sensed that the engine wasn't actually moving.

"The next morning we went out on the Track-Shifter, after a pleasant breakfast served by the relief cook. They said Clyde's hair was somewhat white when he called for his check; but it probably wasn't any more than grayish." I'm really glad I saved this stuff from Will; I'm not sure if anyone will believe most of it. Will's answer would be, " it's all true – except the stuff that isn't."

This next section was Will's final battle with what he called the " Forces Under Central Kontrol of the – US Cold-Hot-War- Corp of Anti-Freedom; or FUCK the – US Cold- Hot-War -Corp of Anti-Freedom." This section title, " Hell-No-I-Won't-Go !! " comes from a strident cry, by men facing the Draft, that grew into a defiant chant by multitudes of protesters at demonstrations across the country. It was like a wailing steam engine whistle that tried to wake America from the nightmare of war hysteria and fanatical patriotism.

Nuclear University Comparative Literary Evaluation and Review

By Geoffry Chancre

Prologue to the Catastrophe Tales

Whan that the Bureaucrat with his bacterial showers,

Hath perced to the root of all trees and flowers,

And bathed everything in such liquors that,

Doth kill and maim the lice and rat;

Whan the breath of the bomb hath passed over all,

And withered the crops and the stock in their stalls.

And the sun shines through the irradiated skies,

And small birds sing with burned-out eyes;

Than all folks longen on pilgrimages to go:

"Get the hell away from the cities, before the radiation snow!"

HELL NO—I WON'T GO !!!
(Up Front With the SDS)

Journal of May 4th, 1970:

I resume my vagabond educational career once more. It seems that I cannot escape the clinging tentacles of ivy creeping up walls. Whether as a theater manager, cook on a fishing boat, working for the railroad, or living on a homestead in Alaska, I always seem to gravitate back to what Ginsberg called, the " Think Pad."

Joe was the main cause of my return. I was working on my homestead, getting the last logs up on the cabin, planning out the roof structure, and thinking about going moose hunting. Then this cryptic letter, bearing three of my forwarding addresses, appeared:

Hey Kilroy,

You can't hide up there among the Polar bears, while the Atomic Man roams the streets down here. Fear, and the war In Southeast Asia, are spreading like radioactive fallout. Don't ask what your country can do to you; come and help us stop it from doing to others. We are at Western Washington College, Bellingham, down in a bunker. We better stop this insane government before it kills us all. It's Hell down here. (you know I always try to sugar coat it.) – – Joe.

College life, however, has changed since my last stretch. I saw a slogan in the Northwest Passage, a campus newspaper: "

War is good for the economy. Invest your son." Now if you are under 26, and your grades drop, they might literally have you shot. Doug , one of us, had his grades go bad shortly after I got here, and he was gone. Even the graffiti is grimmer, like a bit in the john at the Kulshun Tavern; it was a little one-liner that took me clear back to the days of backyard fallout shelters and, Konelrad. In an insidiously quiet voice, it said " The Bomb Knows! "

Guys with long hair and beards, wandering around like deranged tourists snapping pictures at rallies, have become commonplace. The press doesn't try to look like us; they don't want their heads busted. Hoover must've choked when he had to buy all those Nikons. I feel like a veteran of the G. A. R. That's how long ago it seems since I had my first fire-fight with the Federal Bureau of Insecurity.

All my life there have been wars, and rumors of wars. Peace makes lousy rumors; no one believes them . Joe comes tripping down the stairs with a stack of something in his hands. His long, loose, black hair sways opposite his tall frame, and spills over a green sweatshirt.

"Are those the Times that try mens' souls, or just an old stack of Newsweeks? " He stops, removes heavy glasses, and reflects on the pun; "Let's all observe a moment of silence to let that one pass." Then, he continues down into the nest we've rented in Rosie's basement. " Nosy Rosie knows all " is scrawled on our door.

"These are the latest leaflets hot off the mimeo machine. We've heard rumors that Nixon has a private war going in Cambodia; you know falling dominoes. Of course, he and Kissinger would say, ' Ve ver 'chust following orders from Ike! ' You'll see what I mean, when you hear this quote I dug up."

He read aloud the " Great Golfer's " opening drive to the Western Governors 'Conference of 1953, appealing for support of the French in their " Indo-China Policy." Re Ike : " now let us assume that we lost Indochina… The Tin, and Tungsten, and Rubber that we so greatly value would cease coming… so when the United States votes $400 million to help that war, we are not voting a give-away program… we are voting for the cheapest way that we can to prevent the occurrence of something of a most terrible significance to the United States of America.… We need the riches of the Indochinese territory and Southeast Asia."

"Oh Jesus, Ike! When was all of Southeast Asia ours to lose? " I'm shouting out loud and crumpling up the paper. Joe rejoins, " he could've run an ad in the Personals column of the New Your Times: ' Indochina come home; all is forgiven; your father's golf scores arc dropping.' I think…" I interrupt Joe's satirical sketch, to outline the irony of Ike: "American Industry won him World War II . And he was just trying to secure Asia for good business- military stability in 53 ". (No matter that Truman barely left Korea with his ass that very year .)

"Creeping Communism was Ike's cross to bear, so he used the Marine Diplomatic Corp in places like Nicaragua and Lebanon (Lebanon Lebanon, here we come) ." And Joe comes back with "and yet he wound up warning us of the Military-Industrial Complex! " So I add, " it was the Fearful Fifties, Joe, followed by the Sick Sixties -- with Sputnik, and the missile derby – ' No nukes is good nukes ' – that pays you back for ignoring the Times-Newsweek crack." Joe's exit line : " I'm going over to the Students for a Democratic Society table, and drop off these leaflets; you know, like they do in Nham.

I return to my Journal of the plague years. Several times during my life I've received deranged glimpses of what Camus talks about as a "dark wind from the future" blowing toward "

The Stranger." I'd say it's reached gale force, now; it may just sweep away the whole house of golf scorecards.

Cold winds and missiles remind me of a tableau of Christmas past frozen into my memory cells: December 24th 1962 – a blizzard guaranteed a white Christmas for all, and axle deep drifts for my vintage V W Bug. Stopping to beat ice from the windshield wipers kept me awake on a lonely interstate, high in the Cascade Mountains of Washington. Bing Cosby echoed across the radio waves, crooning the virtues of whiteness (He lives in California, and probably wouldn't know a snow shovel from a shit fork.)

Suddenly, a sobering voice interrupted Silent Night: " ladies and gentlemen, we have just received a message from our Distant Early Warning Radar Network in Alaska . An unidentified flying object has been picked up crossing the Polar Cap, headed for the North American continent. A squadron of Strategic Air Command fighter jets has been scrambled for visual identification. We will have word from the wing commander at any moment… ."

My body temperature dropped below life support level. I pulled over while trying to keep my grip on the wheel, and the world.   " This is it! They've done it! The bastards have finally done it! On Christmas

Eve, God how grotesque! " I visualized a global "Atomic Bullet " scenario; but the punch line was too ghastly to envision.

"Capt. Mercury, if you can hear me, would you please describe what you have located? " The radio bleated on.: " Right Mel, were over the Arctic Ocean, north of Canada, and a strange sight we see. It looks like a sleigh and, I see six, seven, eight, reindeer; and there's a driver cracking his whip. They should be over North America soon – Merry Christmas, Mel, and to all a good night."

I turned the radio off, got out and peed in the snow bank, shaking more than just my dick. The mere threat of that light, " brighter than a thousand suns," should have been enough to illuminate the handwriting on the wall for me to read. But, it took Atomic Al, Kennedy's death, and LBJ's life – all culminating in this insane reign of Vietnam war terror and ignorance – to make me recognize the message: it was a wail of desperation, a final plea for relief from the cold, deafening silence.

I remember most of the guys in my Basic Training outfit being scared green of war – but none of us opened our mouths. We just scribbled our complaints on shit-house walls. The Fearful 50s were well named. (Kurt enters the subterranean chambers – quietly, quietly he may not yet perceive us.) " You still down here, Will ? What the hell are you doing, translating ' Notes From The Underground ' into Sanskrit? " Kurt, bearded, beaded, baffled, bored squats on my bunk.

"No, I'm rewriting ' War and Peace' as a modern-day allegory, sort of updating the symbols: the US Marines as the War Corps- versus college students as the Peace Corps – the non- war to end all non- wars! A struggle for the hearts, and minds, and livers, and lungs,… ." I can see he missed my last semantic U-turn.

"Yeah, yeah, right - on, you really have your shit together, Will. Speaking of shit, you got any? " " I see you've quit smoking the stuff they can tax, Kurt. Good, the tobacco tax just goes for guns-and butter. And we know what LBJ greases with that butter. You will be a healthy and high patriot, Kurt. Sorry but I don't use it." " Groovy – hang loose Will. And remember " – he raises two fingers in the Churchill victory sign – " Peace! "

"Somewhere, sometime Kurt. But I fear that war is a reoccurring pandemic, and we can't seem to find the vaccine. I saw a bit of graffiti yesterday that gave me chills. It said: ' God is alive and living in a small South American country – and wants you to send guns!' " " I don't get it Will; it was probably just some dude on a bad acid trip. See you. I'm going over to get my picture taken by the FBI at the SDS stand." Exit Kurt, very photogenic.

The 60s were a trial. However, I believe that, after 10 years and three presidents, the verdict is finally coming in. Even though there seems to be more tunnel at the end of the light, the 70's may actually convict the guilty. I saw eloquent testimony, one of many copies, plastered on the library bulletin boards. An enlarged copy of a document officially titled: " Notice of Order to Report for Induction" summoned the named youth to endorse the defendant's case. But, a defiant hand had scrawled across the document's pasty face in large letters – " HELL NO I WON'T GO! " Obviously aimed at the Bureau of Kratz.

Minus glasses, and breathing hard, Joe stumbles down the stairs. " Will-dammit!- Will! " Joe's hair looks even blacker against his pale face. He slumps on the stairs hanging onto the rail. " They've done it-they've finally done it-like in Mexico! " " What the hell's happening Joe? " My pulse is hitting probably 200. It must be the big one, Nuke City – my 50s reflexes always take over in a crisis. Probably comes from having crawled under so many desks during Air Raid drills. " What about Mexico? "

"IT'S KENT STATE!!!" Joe is shouting. My voice starts rising, " what the hell does that have to do with Mexico? " He jumps up, " KENT STATE, Ohio! It came over the TV at the Student Union. Ohio National Guardsmen shot down dead 4, unarmed student demonstrators on the campus, today! " Joe screams. It tastes once again like biting into green apples, and getting the Third, Eye, and an engine whistle screaming in my head… . " What's happening Joe? Is it 1984 already? Or have we regressed to the 30s in Germany? ”   I'm holding my head with both hands.

Joe rises and starts up the stairs; “ I don't know, Will. There's a candle-light vigil starting in Red Square, over by the library – how ironic, Red Square! There'll be student vigils all over the country, probably even the world, I hope… .” “ I'll get my raincoat, Joe. Let me add one last thing here.”   I write, “ Dear Diary, will return later – I hope. “

LASSIE AND TIMMY WON'T GO TO WAR

(First, Timmy does not fall down a well--Lassie does. And Timmy gets a new dog. And the world falls into chaos) To be the "good man," as he was always pictured , Jesus must've had a dog, even if the Bible never said so. That's how Karl had it figured when he was a child. Several flop- eared, barking candidates for perpetual motion had romped through a rural childhood behind, ahead of, and all around Karl. In his imagination, endless, damp northern forests echoed to the hunting call of one he called Wolf.

And then one day, a hound appeared and, with Karl's parents' permission, became a beloved companion that he naturally named Wolf. The dog always raced up the trail ahead of him, to hide in the green, shadowy sword ferns, and burst out in an ambush of tail wagging mock- combat. But, the great, shaggy body disappeared – in the boy Karl's fantasies – to roam the high hills as leader of his pack once more.

After a sadness involving Duke, a pup who wandered under the wheels of a car, Karl became hesitant to form a friendship with anything four-legged. But, the puppy's brown eyes and comic expressions were too much to resist. Kip and Karl –Karl and Kip, the Yin and Yang of mans' age-old relationship with dogs. There was a crisis when Kip tangled with an ancient fur trap, left out in the woods. The Vet said, without a foot, he should probably be put down. But Karl pleaded with his folks, and spent six months changing bandages, applying medicine, and helping Kip learn to walk again with a rubber shoe.

They shared the same room, the same food (when Mom wasn't looking,) and always the same woods. With Kip nearly one hundred percent, the partners ranged far beyond the dark forests, up into the hills, and valleys, where the legendary Wolf surely led his wild brothers. But Kip was the main dog now. Karl still occasionally wakes up from the terror- filled nightmare of water closing over his face; and he instinctively reaches for the furry lump, no longer at the foot of his bed.

A rafting expedition began with cold, morning water lapping over his toes, and damp mist rising from the summer shore- line. It ended as a lesson in mortality and devotion for Karl. The boy, who had just learned to swim, paddled his log raft beyond the shallows, into deep water. Sunshine sprinkled across wind ripples that made a path to adventure. Karl pulled against the slow-moving deadweight of water soaked logs, while Kip barked a cadence that echoed off the forested hills . Boy and dog bent to the task they were born for.

Cloud shadows ghosted across his craft, and a breeze engulfed him in coolness. Karl stood up and reached for his life jacket hanging on the makeshift mast – and suddenly the water rose up to engulf him. Clammy forces made his legs feel near-useless, drawing him down. He shrieked and water snakes instantly filled his mouth. As he came up thrashing, Kip stood on the raft gazing at him with ears stiff, head cocked at a questioning angle.

Then above him, in the world of light that represented safety, one corner of Karl's frozen mind saw a dark shape thrashing toward him. Barely breaching the surface, Karl frantically sucked in life, and exhaled cruel, gurgling death. The force that seized his shirt from behind caused Karl to instinctively flail the water faster. He and the force sank; but together they rose much more quickly. It churned the deadly water with wild strokes, with only three good feet, and together they kept them both barely afloat.

He only felt the pain of his thrashing arm striking the logs much later. Seizing wet bark, he kicked and clawed his way aboard the island haven, then grabbed Kip's collar and heaved till he fell over. Karl lay with his eyes closed staring at the dark vein patterns the sun made through his lids. He coughed, gasped, coughed again, and suddenly felt a cold nose on his face.

Boy and dog lay shivering and panting. The human child was reborn into a world much more dangerous than it had been before sunrise that morning. Kip was a hero, but only to Karl; such a story would have surely resulted in a dry-docking of all vessels by the Admiral. But, the dog needed the adulation of only one person.

Now grown to five- foot nine, muscular yet quiet for his 25 years, Karl doesn't think very often of Kip's last days. Life remembered is always better without tragic partings. Kip's muzzle, then the entire coat, turned gray and his body became spare. He lay in the sun on the concrete walk, and cooked throughout that Summer; the fall rains kept him constantly by the fireplace. He would slowly raise his head and squint at strange sounds, but no longer went to investigate.

Once the great shaggy friend had snatched Karl from a potential non-life. And Karl realized he could not return the gift. He carried his great friend to the car, his arms clutching the frail, hairy body, his legs weak, not wanting to move forward. He whispered " goodbye my old friend – I won't forget you…." He never has; he never will.

Karl slowed down before the poster in the Student Union Building. One large black word triggered his pause reflex: " CANINE; " It caught at his brain, and caused him to focus on the rest of the words. He rarely read the stuff they put up – it was usually "anti- war " this and "stop the draft " that. But, the title "Army Canine Combat Demonstration, " moved him to read further. " K-9 Combat and Security Techniques – library lawn – 2 PM, Saturday, August 15, 1970."

Karl sped up, late for his Lit. Class as usual. But after class, he slowly drifted home, brooding, thinking of bits and pieces of stories he now recalled of "killer dogs" being trained for Vietnam . Dust rose with the heat as he passed the clamor and splashing of the community pool. Arms and legs thrashing the water suddenly brought into focus his memory: he felt the gagging waves closing over him, and a set of jaws gripping his shirt, while both swam for their lives. He cut across the railroad tracks in a haze of creosote and cooked out diesel fumes.

Scoopy met him at the fence, and followed down to the corner gate. She padded along on silent paws, head down-- but not cowed – dark eyes scanning everywhere. Lean ropes of muscles, alert ears, brownish gray, short hair, and snowshoe like paws, showed the trained eye her wild antecedents. Her head raised in a furtive stare, Karl caught the flash of the wild in her deadpan gaze. Head lowered momentarily in submission, she rose on hind legs to place her forepaws carefully on his shoulders. Nose buried in his chest, she snuffled him. He tousled her coarse hair and ears; " for being half wolf, you sure aren't very standoffish. But you want in the house, don't you? " She dropped to all fours, and loped up the path and steps.

Mrs. Diesman loved dogs, but she had been uncertain about the wolfish ways of the Alaskan Husky that he showed her when he applied for the room. Karl carefully demonstrated Scoopy's submissive nature, and over tea he regaled her with tales of training Scoopy to become the leader of a dog team on his homestead in Alaska.

He threw in the story of running the sled on a frozen creek, breaking through the ice, and getting his feet wet. Scoopy put it in high gear to get the team home to a thawing , woodstove fire. It was all true, but it embarrassed him to tell it. Scoopy dozed by his feet, slanted eyes shut, tail always curled under a naturally, semi- tensed body.

As they ate dinner that night, Karl chatted with Scoopy about his plans for the coming Saturday. " It'll give you some exercise, and a chance to show them what a real working dog is all about. This heat will be hard on you; but we'll make it short, and you can lay under the sprinklers." The next morning, Karl dug out a harness he had brought with him. He braided the tug line from an old rope, and lashed it to a kids large wagon he had borrowed. After he laid out the gear, Scoopy began dancing around when she saw the line and harness; her eyes shone. Karl calmed her down, then slipped on the harness, and hooked the end of the harness to the " sled."

Knowing the first two blocks were going to be a wild ride, he started down the dirt road paralleling the railroad bed. At the command " Hike," Scoopy arched her back, dug in with all 4 feet, and lunged forward. The wagon jumped, almost upsetting. She picked up her gait, and Karl held on as the wheels crunched and clanked across the dirt and stones. The great lean body moved in an ancient rhythm –front feet, hind feet – open/ close – open/ close – a gait for covering Arctic distances on cold, winter nights.

As she calmed down and smoothed out, Karl spoke directions: " Whoa-easy, okay Hike on." They proceeded up the avenue, gathering interested looks. " Ghee-Ghee! " The trained ears hearing the signal, the body executed a perfect right turn. " Haw-Scoop-Haw! " The flying feet swung left and onto the campus main drag.

When Karl stopped in front of the library, he got out her pan and drew water from a sprinkler tap. As she lapped, Karl observed the library lawn with its newly erected rectangular fencing. Within were transport cages containing large dogs, one a Shepherd, the other a Doberman Pincer. Several men in military garb, sweltering in fatigues and boots, strolled around smoking cigars and eyeing Karl and Scoopy.

"We will now demonstrate some obedience maneuvers used to train these precision canines. Sgt.Sloan, will you proceed, please? " The sergeant put a Shepherd called Ranger through its paces. Ranger responded with atomaton reflexes to hand signals, leaping over barriers and running through mazes. Then, an officer type adjusted the volume of his bullhorn to address the scattered crowd lining the fence. " We will now demonstrate the security maneuvers."

Meanwhile, passing students were surprised by unusual requests from a quiet talking guy with a wolf -looking dog hooked to a wagon. " Just stand here, please okay? " Karl placed one student every 20 feet forming a line of five people. Then he brought his " team" toward the first uncertain volunteer. " Now Scoop-easy-slow-Ghee… ." As they passed to the right of the first human "pylon," Karl called " Haw-Haw – that's it " and the Husky swung left between the next two students in line.

As they passed the third, hesitant marker, Karl spoke again, "Ghee,Ghee," and they passed between the next students. Now the audience understood what was happening. They watched, fascinated, as the wagon and its passenger threaded down through the slalom course, the great dog pulling and panting. And then they began cheering! The military observed in silence – then they brought out their big guns.

Kain, the Doberman, shifted his weight from paw to paw, and glanced around nervously. Ears erect, back arched, eyes blank, unblinking , Kain prepared for the main event – his trainer held the command lead at arms length. Suddenly, from behind a plywood screen, a Halloween figure rushed out firing a blank pistol. The trainer, dressed in heavily padded body armor and gloves, lurched toward the man with the dog! Kain hurled himself at the wood-be attacker, locking onto his gun arm and dragging the fat ,flailing form down.

It had all happened so fast, the audience was stunned. Kain hovered over the victim, maintaining a thrust-for-the throat position, while the other trainer removed the pistol from the padded hand. As the bullhorn praised the animal and trainer, another sight suddenly distracted the audience. The young man and his splendid wolf dog walked around and around the perimeter of the fence, both quiet and casual.

Karl wears a sandwich- board sign, heavy and hot under the baking sky. On front and back it simply says: " My Dog Saves Lives." And Scoopy wears a light, cloth sign draped over her back, like a set of racing silks. It says: " Yankee Imperialist Dogs Go Home." They walked the fence for a while stopping to rest, drink, and relax in the shade – both wishing it were minus 10 below zero and a full, moonlit Arctic night.

Editor's Final Note: (Yippee, The Horror, The Horror is over)

In the year of our Ford, 1974: Huxley was right on; Orwell was a decade late.

Our boys are home, but not the last man. The long night isn't over for the "POW's, or the "MIA's." The War produced something grotesquely original: a US President Missing In Action; it's all just water over the gate for Nixon, folks.

The executions at Kent State made a temporary MIA out of Will. In that same night, he reported what he called "the final straw man." Rc Will: " Joe and I went to the Vigil in Red Square. There was a great crowd, a huge number of candles wavered in the dark, and an ecric silence. It was wonderful, until there was a commotion just off the Square. Joe and I went to check it out.

"The S D S (Students for a Democratic Society) a left-wing group, were manning a stand, as they had for several weeks, handing out anti-war pamphlets. They flew a Viet Cong Flag above it. The S R E (Students for Responsible Expression) a right- wing group, were protesting the stand.

"Apparently, the SRE decided that responsible expression included attempting to tear down the stand and flag. A hassle began, and led to the flagpole being torn down and broken. Just as we got there, two people were knocked to the pavement; turns out they were innocent civilians (like always happens.) The cops came, and the wounded were taken to the hospital.

"We got this report from a friend – a nurse in the emergency room. She told us: the injured reported to the cops that three men were trying to tear down a flag, and they got hit in the head with the pole." Joe said, " we have eyewitnesses; let's see them twist that around to blame us." The College tried to hold everyone responsible, and it wound up with a huge, divided crowd in Red Square confronting each other. Again the cops came, and the crowds dispersed; it could have been a hideous melee.

"Ian Trivette, head of the SDS, called a meeting at the Student Union. While he was speaking, an SRE guy tried to interrupt him. Trivette yelled, ' your civil rights end – where mine begin!! ' The whole thing made Will an M I A from the Battle of Red Square, and the Movement. He disappeared, and some of his friends thought Hoover was behind it.

But, in two months we heard from Will, working on an oil rig in Alaska. Will's letters from that period conveyed a clear message: he was through winning the battle and losing the war. He went over the hill, anti—anti– war in his usual inverted style. When I made my near fatal blunder in 1971, Will was on the phone to me, chewing my ass off, like I really needed that in Boot Camp.

After our final – nearly final in the real sense – adventure together in 1972, Will sent me these journals. He asked me to " either make sense out of this chaos, or chaos out of this sense, which ever sounds more reasonable." Will – Reasonable-- it's an oxymoron. For instance, consider the following letter sent to me by my brother while I was awaiting shipment to the Grand Adventure. Because I didn't listen to Will closely, I never really understood the war until I was in it.

If he had sent me the letters like this, before I signed up for the Army, there's a possibility I might've begun to understand. This letter is addressed to Bob Dylan:

Dear Bob,

The "100 Years War" can be encapsulated in the following manner: small, factional armies roamed Europe in a constant state of attack; large masses of civilians scurried about in a continual state of retreat; the citizens, thinking themselves to be running from the fray, in reality were merely advancing toward another battle. A cinematic view of world history; the wars of man as the longest continual re-run ever staged. (If you look too closely, you might see yourself on the screen, today.) I'm sorry Bob, I cannot agree with you. The " Times " do not seem to be "A Changin." – – Yours-Will Tully

When I got here, to Vancouver in 72', I was still carrying his letters. Sardonic humor was Will's searchlight; he used it to reveal the darkness of the times. I eventually ran across its best illustration in the journals; so I bring it to you – Seattle: General William Westmoreland addresses the Western Governors Conference attempting to explain Vietnam. He is accompanied by 200 really odd folks shoving on the hotel banquet doors, while chanting "Waste More Land! Waste More Land! Waste More Land! " Suddenly, the double doors give way, as the horrified Maitre De faces the unruly mob. The protesters are silenced by the situation: rulers and ruled are suddenly face-to-face, equal under the terms of direct redress of abuse of power. Will leaps forward and presses a dollar into the hand of the astonished head waiter, calling out in a loud voice: " table for 200 my good man; the true governors are here! "

Let that stand as a tribute to the man's style. After reading Will's stories, and the novella entitled "Dog Tags," I understand the journals, the Dylan letter and others, all of it. Especially clear to me now are Will's comments about political assassinations in America: " From 1965 to 1970, five major political figures were taken out by hit men. America became a banana republic, just like that: just like Jack, just like Martin, just like Bobby, just like Medgar, just like Malcom, just like Kilroy, just like us, Fil."

Editing these journals is my way of saying thank you to Will for being there. It's a specific thank you for his part in our near- final adventure as recorded in "Dog Tags." The story is Will's way of saying thanks to our father, John Wester, and to me.

Nuclear University Comparative Literary Evaluation and Review

By Robert Fission

Stopping by Embers on a Radiant Evening

> Whose woods these were I think I know.
> His house was in the village though;
> He'll never see me stopping here
> To watch his woods smolder and glow.
> My little horse stands halt and blind.
> No farmhouse, woods, or billboard sign
> Between ground zero, horse and me;
> The darkest flash ever seen by mankind.

By Carbon Sandburnt

Fog of War

> Radiation comes
> On little cat feet;
> It sits looking
> Over harbor and city,
> On glowing haunches,
> And then kills all.

DOG TAGS–A NOVELLA

"Mighty indeed are the marks and monuments of our Empire which we have left. Future ages will wonder at us, as the present age wonders at us now... . For our adventurous spirit has forced an entry into every sea and into every land; and everywhere we have left behind us everlasting memorials of good done to our friends, or suffering inflicted on our enemies."

Pericle's Funeral Oration

Thucydide's, History of the Peloponnesian Wars

Notes of A Native Son-of-a-Bitch

Chapter 1

Once more, I studied the gray, metal discs dangling from a key circle that was a former hand grenade pin-ring . I had thrown the hand grenade away many years ago. Had I known that these dog tags were going to make a much greater explosion in my life, I might've pitched them out the window into Cook Inlet, Alaska's oil lagoon.

One of the harmless looking discs said, " Will Tully – US 29011227 – T 58 – O – Episcopal." That was the Army; I had listed my religion as Buddhist. The second tag, nearly 20 years older, said, " Jim Klee – US – 1181325 – T 42 – Lutheran." Knowing Jim like I had, I'll bet he put down for religion "fast money." But I'll also bet the Army was the same in 42', as it was in 58'.

As always, feeling that obscene notch in the rounded end of the tag gave me the momentary sensation of having it pounded between my front teeth. It was accompanied by a replay of Sgt. Lopez: " that's what that notch is there for; don't be squeamish about driving it in your buddies front teeth; it may be the only way his parents will get the right body. "

I dropped them into a beat-up, greenish duffel bag, with the very faded Ed Tully on it, and scanned the bunk cubicle one last time. I kicked the empty locker shut, and shouldered my burden. Out on the heliport deck, I watched the hands putting another stick of pipe on the drill stem and starting another trip down the hole. Lynn, the tower man high above, waved and I waved back. He and I had had some great times in Anchorage on our off times.

The Gray- green water was filled with ice floes that ground around and banged on the stilt legs of the oil rig, moving back and forth with the tide. Sometimes the ice hitting the legs might almost knock you out of bed. The wind whipped around the derrick tower with an arctic bite. Waving to Red the tool-push, I instinctively ducked under the wickering rotor blades, tossed the duffel bag and guitar case into the chopper, and climbed in. A lurch, then weightlessness, an upward rush, and the platform dropped away below us.

Through the insulated, iso- thermal plane window I studied distant human forms lingering around the airport taxi strip. Bent and broken natives, Aleuts, Athabascans, Eskimos, freezing their asses off, solemnly observing landings and take- offs. Workers in ivory, drinkers of poison, makers of tourist trinkets, milling around behind the hurricane fencing, expecting no- one, expected no- where. They waved, then a sudden thrust, a dizzying rush, and Anchorage International disappeared behind a screen of ice- fog.

At several intervals, I got a glimpse of the coastline of South- East Alaska, with the chain of coastal islands that form the famous Inside Passage. Those old timers really went through hell, during the gold rush. Two or three weeks, to cover the same territory I'll cover in three hours. (But, they had the trip to experience and remember, a speck of gold, maybe that was worth it?")

Just like it was worth it for the original settlers who came out to Washington, when it was Oregon Territory. They had one hell of a time on that Oregon Trail. But when they got out there, and got set up, they led pretty good lives, according to old John. The way he tells it, Midway must have been quite a place back then. (Now, it's all gone, maybe John, too.)

That set me to recalling the newspaper blurbs the old man had sent: "A modern wonder of the world..." "The largest concrete dam ever conceived by man..." " Another milestone in the history of this great Country... ." Also, there were accompanying photos: a meaty smile behind a number 10 shovel, as "Mr. Big" turns the first earth. (It's probably the first time he ever had to use a spade . He should be made to dig the whole damn thing by hand.)

Then, there were the old man's letters: his descriptions of the final exodus from the old town – Midway, on the sunny Columbia – sinking beneath the waves. And, behind all of these recollections lingered the thought of John Wester standing against the tide: behind him the Bureaucrats; before him the water. Sorta like little brother Fil : behind him the Brass; before him a dog-tag between the teeth. (Why didn't I do more for him than make that call? I just sat on my ass, up there in that igloo, while he marched into that mess.) The old man's last letter was a coded message. I got it out of my pocket and re-read the part about his medical check- up being touchy, and wishing he could see Fil and me again. It was the way he implied Fil's duty to his family coming before duty to country. If I knew Ed Tully, at all, he was thinking more than he was saying.

Accompanying my suspicions were numerous drinks served by the smiling goddess. I did notice that the smile grew thinner as the alcohol grew thicker. Finally, glacial expressions began accompanying cool offers of hot coffee. Without any visible effort on my part, I had descended from first class to last caste; I was a one man airliner leper colony.

Carefully walking down the aisle, I seemed to be getting the once- over from everyone. Passing by the stewardesses' mirror, it suddenly occurred to me why I was receiving such close scrutiny. There were not many red bearded, long- haired, cowhide jacketed hombres in those parts. With my leather hat, I looked like something off the Buffalo range. As I flushed my drinks, and my thoughts, down the stainless steel tube, a metallic voice resonated from the walls.

"We are entering the Seattle area approach pattern, folks; please return to your seats and we'll be landing soon. Thank you." (There is no privacy even in the privy.) I shambled down the wet, metal stairs, onto the glazed tarmac. Seattle – rain – what's one without the other? The terminal bar was filled with GI's and tobacco smog.

"That's quite a beard you have there, partner; did you just come in from the Klondike? I'm from around here, myself; may I welcome you to our fair city with a drink? " I thanked him, then managed to reduce my field of vision to the coolness between my hands, drowning out the clinking glassware and droning bar talk. I began an interior monologue: (Call the bus station – call a cab – call it a day – de ol' plantation am flooded – full fathom five lies over his head – what about John's cabin… ?)

I bought the Welcome Wagon a round, then departed. Dropping off the stool, I hoisted the bag and guitar case, and slouched toward the door. My feet hit the floor okay, but my head kept screwing up the rhythm. A nice, steady rat-drownder maintained the city's tradition of Water- World. A line of cabs, vintage models all, stretched into the shadowed area- way.

As I approached the first one, a cabbie hailed me from about the fourth in line: " Hey, throw your stuff in the rear, and let's go! " I moved down the line and obeyed. He opened the door, I shoved my burden into the interior, and he shoved me into the front seat. As he climbed behind the wheel, he called to the first cabbie in line, " he's a friend of mine, okay? "

I stared into an inquisitive face – its odor of grape gum mingling with Eau-de-Taxi – then it grinned and spoke: " Will

Tully, you young squirt, Boy Howdy! " A hand appeared, Les Everman's hand. I took it, shook it and sank back. " Les, what in the hell are you doing in a cab, at the Sea Tack Airport, at whatever the hell time it is, talking to me? "

As the engine croaked, he spoke, " that's a long one, Will. Let's hit a café and we'll go into it." We rolled along the darkened freeway, with occasional streetlights drifting in and out of the drizzle. The rain, the engine's drone, the soft seat, the windshield wipers' measured licking (all this and the meter isn't clicking and the time-bomb in my pickled brain is barely ticking – luxury.)

"I was just coming out the other door, when I saw you headed for the hack stand. I was pretty sure it was you, but I had to get up close what with the mountain man look." Les shifted into second and pulled up to an all-nighter. We went in, picked up coffee, and made our way to a booth. " Been a long time since I set eyes on you, Will." "Yeah, it's good to see you too Les. How's Shirley? " "Fine, fine. Here we are in the big city. I'm just pushing hack for the hell of it; I really don't have to work, you know." He grinned, then stared down into his cup.

"It sounds like you're doing well Les. But-ah- why did you leave the valley? I mean, I thought they were going to relocate everyone who… " He looked up, "– oh, that old outfit in Midway – I got tired of seeing the same faces, you know. So we packed up and decided to live under the lights for a while." He waved his cigarette in a tired gesture, sweeping away the entire scene with a flick of an ash.

Somewhere, a siren grew from a thin wail to an angry growl. Les' hands shook, spilling coffee on the endearments carved into the tabletop; I was thankful no Kilroy. " Damn! We got to jawin' and I missed my E T A. Let's get you to your bus."

He strode towards the door – "catch me next time, O K Sam? " We wheeled into the rumbling night.

Shifting into high gear, Les' narrative out raced his rapping valves: " I told that damn dispatch I had one for the Greyhound Depot. They have the estimated time the trip should take, and if I don't report pretty close to that, they notify the patrols. That squad car might be for me." With one hand on the wheel, and the other on the radio mike, tersely, he pled his case: " This is 138. One for Greyhound was 'D and D;' it's OK now, call off the dogs! " He saluted the dashboard with the universal one finger, while shouting over the engine.

"I had to tell them you were Drunk and Disorderly." We lurched around a Volkswagen that dutifully squatted at the stoplight. " They'll probably hit me with a penalty for reporting late anyway, dammit!" Les peered into the rearview mirror; " if they saw that red light I just ran, there goes my permit. Jesus, Will, when you see your old man, tell him to stay put – friggin' Corp of Engineers and their dam!-- Probably thought we were just a buncha' hicks. I even helped build the son of a bitch; I figured it was going to flood my place anyway."

Entering the Greyhound approach pattern, we banked into an exit, with the tires moaning and the gears winding down. While the buildings slowed down, Les' crescendo narrative sped up, and we set down in front of the bus terminal. " Thank you Les, thank you – I'll tell the old man hello from you – thank you! Here, let me give you something." Wiping his forehead with a shaking hand, he waved it away; "nah, this ones on me Will."

Opening the door, I pushed the bags out, and straightened up. As he pulled away, Les honked. I waved, then turned to meet the blank stare of an idling coach, its headlights cold, unblinking. For once, I was more than willing, I was elated to leave the driving to them.

Grit – that has always been my impression of bus stations. Many times a simple roadside café, with an elongated dog on a tin sign, becomes a logical extension of its parent terminals in big cities: an oasis of grime and loneliness in the howling landscape, rife with the medicinal brotherhood of man . I preferred standing in the loading zone, to enduring the waiting room. A fine, cold spray swept through the high -arched cavern; diesel fumes and damp pigeons rose into the canopy with each departing car.

A scruffy character, with a satchel and horn case, paused before me. A tall form in a beat-up raincoat and long, wool scarf, he stopped; I turned away; he passed on. He was going to tell me about how he needed bus fare to make this gig he was playing, and he couldn't hock the horn. Front seat, top-side, on a Greyhound Scenicruiser, with windows in front of us, that was my idea of traveling, especially after years of hitchin'. I took the inside seat, and a Navy man chose me for a seatmate. My luck was holding.

Across the aisle, the musician who had paused before me on the loading platform shared my ideas of class. It was really going to be old home week. Water swirled over the blue-green window ahead of us; wavering streetlights slid by, overhead. In a series of rumbling lurches, we wound through Seattle, the Mecca of the great American Migration to the Pacific North West.

The ancient mariner, beside me, was making sounds like a drowning storyteller wanting me to throw him a verbal lifeline . He finally lapsed into a sustained monologue that I tried to ignore, but he prevailed: " I just got out – three fuckin' years on the Enterprise – never again, no sir! I'm heading for home, and they ain't never gonna see me near anything wetter than beer. Boy, we used to say that we would strap a life- jacket on our backs, and walk in- land until somebody asked us what that thing was; and we would stop, right there! Ha!-Ha! You ever heard that one?" "I think some old Greek with an oar... " I tried.

"Hey, here we go; we're out of the shitty city. It's clear sailin' from here to Spokane, and then Cour de Lene, and then Missoula. I change there for... ." I gave it one more try, " Ithaca?" "Nope. I don't know where that is. From Missoula I head North to Omik, that's Buffalo in Blackfoot. I'm related to Indians, a ways back; my great-grandmother was a princess." I nodded. He went on, " Yeah, last time I was back there was in 69', " he added; " that place never changes though... ." He plunged onward.

I managed to keep my head up, and eyes half open. The plot wasn't too hard to follow, but I got caught ad-libbing, every now and then. Soon, his voice harmonized with the drone of the engine. Then, another voice, one that demanded attention, emerged from my loggy mind: (poor Les, sitting in that cab somewhere, waiting for the next fare to stick a gun in his neck. Maybe the old man can tell me more about what happened. Hell, dad's letters always made the dam sound like a bad joke, not really serious.)

I was dimly aware that the sailor had impressed another audience. His new listener, the scarecrow musician, was attempting a bit of up-staging, but Navy was giving no quarter: "Yep – the Enterprise is a big ship. She could cruise the Tropics for four months, without..." The horn man wailed " I just returned from a long voyage, myself. I've been to the South Seas. It's beautiful there – they believe in free love, and everyone lives in communal bliss..."

"Oh yeah? We put into Hawaii once. Boy they got some great places there – nice girls..." the sailor countered. Again the horn, " we all loved one another, and all mankind..." As the musical pantheists extolled the brotherhood of man, a small glow flared up, behind him. Sorority-Sue was practicing her hard-won right to smoke in public places. As the dueling monologue between the Navy and the horn man lulled, a dry acrid smoke crept over the seatback.

I was communing with the inner man, when someone across the aisle coughed – a small, dry sound. From my mining experience, I had come to realize how the smallest of sparks can light a fuse. " What happened, did you light the filter on that thing? " Horn guy gagged. " Yes, I guess I must have – it's so dark..." she pleaded. " Well, how about opening your window? I mean the rest of us have to breathe you know." His doctrine of universal understanding obviously did not extend to public transportation. "My window won't open, I'm sorry." She was politic, but leery of the specter in the wool winding sheet. In lieu of the Marines, the Navy arrived.

"Where I come from, we're more polite to our womenfolk. I'll try to open ours. That okay with you chief?" I was going to point out to our musical voyageur that by kicking the bottom of his window he could procure all the fresh air he needed. But the descendent of the Blackfeet slid our porthole back. "That suit you, Mac? " Re horn-man: " you sound hostile; that's unfortunate. You must have a lot of repressed hostility in you from your long tour..."

He was applying Psych 101. I could've told him he was playing in the wrong key, but our little red brother put it in much plainer terms: " Listen Jack – just knock off the horse -shit. You got your ventilation, so just deal yourself out! " I proceeded to apply his sage advice to myself. Not wishing to view a mobile re- enactment of the Custer massacre, I moved down the dimly lit steps and opened the door to seclusion.

As the narrow door closed, a rendition of the Freud Sonata for night coach was ensuing. " You see there are some things we don't realize are disturbing us, because we want to forget…" The music played on. A good, steady engine drone permeated the walls of my domain; everything was compact, cozy. The light was designed to make reading impossible – basic functions only – life simplified, deodorized, ideal conditions for meditating and shitting.

(I'll have breakfast in Ellensburg, then we head for the Columbia and Newport. A brand-new town – the miracle of government money – I'll bet they even have central sewage. God, I remember that walk to the outhouse; then we got indoor plumbing. Fil and I used to kid the old man about going soft. It sure was great for mom though. She would've been happy at Newport – new people to meet – new customers for the old man – new blood in the old – wonder what keeps the thing going? If Les got hit, the other farmers along the river must've lost a lot of – What?)

A gentle forward motion ensued, then a release, then forward again; air brakes hissed as a voice broke into my W C monologue: " Wenatchee folks; we will be here for 10 minutes; your car is number 737." (There is no sanctuary!) After Wenatchee, I sat in the lower section where slumber prevailed. Above and behind me, a reedy voice sporadically rose and fell. I watched the cold darkness slide by the glass, until the voice faded out.

Chapter 2

Ellensburg – the city of trembling vagrants – with the frosted terminal windows advertising 15° above zero.   I wandered across the marble floors, waiting for the taped voice to announce the car for Newport. Old ladies dozed, clutching their shopping bags in desperation. In one corner, a military coup occupied the embossing machine, reveling in their victory by printing obscene mottos on small metal discs. (I wonder if they will wear them on their dog tags chain?)

Instinctively avoiding the restroom, I took refuge in a secluded corner, and descended into the inner sanctum: (everywhere, people are converging on places like this, or fleeing them, trying to avoid their past, or escape their future. And here I am, after five years, sitting in the same terminal – that word has an ominous connotation – awaiting a return to my origins. Correction, it is only possible for me to go home again with scuba gear – Thomas Wolf never figured on that – but…)

He was lingering before me, apparently studying my guitar case. (Lazarus!) I slowly close my eyes, hoping for the Indians to show up again, knowing that the bus was already on its way to Missoula. " I'm Artie; hey, do you play that thing? " He pointed at the guitar case. The scarf dangled around his knees, bobbing with his Adam's apple;   " hey man, what's happening outside? "

"Nothing is happening outside. It's all inside, man, all inside our heads." I tried to return to privacy. "it's all happening out there, man; let's get us some air, see if we can make some music. " His voice raised several decibels in the slumbering chamber. (I'm always up for some jamming.) I followed him out the door. "I gotta watch for my ride, man," he intoned.

We stepped out into a frizzled of snow falling on the street, but the sidewalk was clear. Shadowy flakes fell out of the bright cones cast by the streetlights, down along the dark canyon of buildings. He set the satchel down, placed the horn case beside it, and began working the latches. " Hope you can follow most cords." He rose with a saxophone, a high-powered sax I was to find out. He adjusted the neck-sling, and took off on "The Saints." I kept the background straight while he warmed up. Then he started wailing, slow, and building the beat. We moved!

We were working our way into "Take Five," when a red, M. G. coupe wrenched itself into the curb . Its still headlights tunneled down the falling curtain of snow. Artie stopped at the refrain, and started packing. The M. G. spoke, " hey – do I know you, or what? " "This is it – I have returned – Reasurgam !" Artie threw his arms up and flailed the burning air. A giant porter in denims and a black beard got out, and grabbed Artie's bags. " I'm Bob Bolstad – just call me balls. " Then Artie turned to me – " you coming with your own people? "

The sanity of the light from the depot windows fell between us in a pale glow on the sidewalk. (This is how I have usually met most of the people worth meeting, like Joe. But, the old man and Rolly need me now.) " I got people who really need me ; another time another place, most likely." "Okay Will, if we see you again, you'll see us again – seems to work that way don't it ? " They left in a cloud of snow.

The bus depot looked even grimmer in the freezing light of day. Choosing a solitary table in the "Chuck Wagon Grill," I waited for my bus call and thought about writing Fil a postcard. That's when I remembered his unopened letter, received just as I was packing up on the rig. It was weeks old, according to the postmark.

"Chaosville – Will – the last word I got, you were still in Alaska, frosting your butt off on an oil   rig. That was just before I bailed out. Where are you now, and why? As to why I am here, in Nahm, I've been asking myself the same question. Every morning it reverberates through my pickled mind: 'Tully, what the fuck you doing here? ' Someday I hope to get an answer; hopefully I'll still be above ground to hear it. Dad says you may be coming home soon. I can forewarn you – be prepared for the worst – before you see Newport. It's no place like home. The phrase 'planned community', on the Corps of Engineers' pamphlet, is gross understatement. The emphasis is on UTILITY.   With dad moving, and starting a new business , and me being another mouth to feed, I made the Beau Geste: I quit school, and joined the Army – some jest… "

A booming voice carried over the clatter of dishes: "the Greyhound coach for Harpers Landing, Newport, (the machine can't remember Midway) Kettle Falls, and the International Boundary is in the final stage of boarding in Lane seven – all aboard ." Gathering up the letter, I stuffed it in my pocket, and hoisted the bag and guitar case, and ran for the loading platform. I settled into my seat, its iron skeleton registering on my tailbone, and resumed Fil's letter.

"… I find that I have the dubious distinction of being the only guy in this company whose hometown no longer exists; it's like being the lone survivor of an extinct race. Some of us, here, are wondering what would happen if Army security wanted to check-up on my background and found that Midway, Washington cannot be located. It became too much for Sgt. York, when a couple of us started explaining these things to him – of course it might've been clearer if we had left out the existential stuff like "non-being" and "potential-to-be." But, we weren't striving for clarity.   Dad took the loss well, and did all right. He got a spot in Newport, because the government forced the sale of the new town site. When you get home, write me about the old man's health, O. K.? He's been writing me stuff I don't like the sound of.- Yours – Kilroy (At least I know at this point he doesn't have a dog tag stuck in his teeth. Why didn't I come home back in 71 and stop him from joining?)

We rolled north, up a familiar stretch of road. Shifting down for each hill, the bus groaned and swayed between high snow burms. Telephone pole shadows slipped under us as we lurched over sanded, compacted snow and ice. An occasional County truck went by, its blade throwing up sparks across the frozen surface. A downshift, and a wheeze of air brakes, announced the river crossing outside Harpers Landing.

As we paused to release an ancient denizen, I saw the skinny, tin dog still drooped from the side of the Harper hotel, the same old pile of faded bricks and blank windows. It hadn't changed much, but it was also below the great Gate; "it's all water over the dam" could become more than a cliché. I recalled fleeting childhood reveries of Harpers Landing as a place where you went to meet folks at the old-fashioned train depot; it was a place of hello's and goodbyes—until the train never came back.

"Newport," the driver's voice cracked over the tinny P. A. system, through the bus darkly. I stepped down into the colding air. Fil was right; it was a place like unhome. I suppose nothing could have prepared me for the new "Turf Bar/Grill." Neon beer signs winked fuzzy red and white halos through the frosted windows. The wind was settling for the night, and stars coming out of the darkening East. The driver helped me with my bags, then hurried into the café.

I paused. Up the street, on the left, a brand-new Chevron station lighted-up the intersection (that must be the old man's place.) I turned to shoulder the bag, and the bus driver reappeared in the doorway. Behind him, a form lingered in the glare of the half opening; a face looked me over with a curious glance and then shut the door from the freezing dark. I turned and started down the greasy sidewalk. Diesel fumes and grinding gears rolled by.

A semi-tractor, idling in the station area- way, devoured two men in its gaping jaws; they dug into the entrails by the glimmer of a drop light. I walked out of the dull glow of mercury vapor, and into the bright, warm oil smell of a tidy office. The place looked more like a store than any garage the old man ever owned: neat stacks of new boxes, and tires in individual racks lined the walls (I'll bet the toilets even smell nice.) "Something I can do for you?" It was polite but neutral. A guy about my age, wearing greasy coveralls, entered the office, and slid the door shut. He rubbed his fingers and motioned for the trucker to hold on .

"I'm wondering if my old man is…" " You're Will ! Boy, Howdy. Ed told us you would morn' likely creep in like this, some night. Just got off that bus, ha? " He introduced himself as Jack Parston, and we shook. Signaling for the trucker to come in, he poured out coffee from a pot on the back of the oil heater. I declined his offer to phone the old man, and said I would surprise him. I dialed, remembering the old man's black hatred for the telephone. He always said, "any damn fool can dial right into my living room, without being invited." "Howdy, Ed here, where are you?" "Hello dad, this isn't just any damn fool ; it's your special damn fool."

On the way to the old man's place, he pointed out the wonders of Newport. My introduction via the bar and station was not altogether representative: there was a drive-in restaurant, boarded up for the winter, in a snow drifted parking lot; functional stores with brick façades, their windows dimly lit; and wonder of wonders, Newport boasted a traffic light – blinking red – never seen in Midway. As we pulled into a driveway between the gap in a rail fence, I got sort of a jolt.

There in the drifted dark glimmered the lighted window of a trailer house.

Moving up the crunching path, we shared my load; he opened the frost stuck door. It wasn't as bad as I expected: the place was all chrome, and metal, and plastic, but the old man had fixed it up like a bachelor's hunting cabin. The frayed bear rug lying on the floor, cold weather and rain gear hanging on the pegs, elk racks holding rifles, all bore the old man's singular stamp. A wood-burning stove flickered away in the living area. The back bedroom was a workshop, with a chainsaw having minor surgery on the bench.

He cleared off the couch in the front room, and I rolled out my sleeping bag. The dog tags clattered out, but I shoved them back to the bottom of the duffel bag. We finished off our coffee, exchanging small talk about the weather, the hunting, and my trip. Most of the furniture was handmade from natural timber (the old boy's kept himself busy as usual.) He looked about the same – no apparent scars from the recent surgery that had cut him off from almost everything that was his past.

"You better take an extra blanket, Will. That fire gets pretty low, and she turns frosty in here." He looked around – " it's a pretty slick outfit – bought it off one of those construction stiffs, after the dam was finished. Best idea I've ever had; just right for me and the little company I keep." He turned out the kitchen light, opened the door and checked the sky, shut the door and headed for his bedroom. "Night Will – sure glad you made it – looks like maybe no more snow for a while. See you in the a.m."

Next morning the old man was up for a while before I came around. A faint light crept in the windows; the room was cozy, warm and steamy. I slid on jeans and wool shirt, padding back to the john barefoot. The old man kidded me about " the new frontiersman " not pissing in a snow bank, just to check the morning temperature. He was in rare form, and the bacon smelled like breakfast.

Afterward, we set out on the grand tour of Newport. It wasn't as bad as Fil made it out. It wasn't Midway, but the people in the supermarket seemed friendly enough. Dad pointed out the trailer park he was in. " Decent enough places for people on retirement, Will. I say it's good: let the old folks off the hook; they paid theirs; these trailers ain't hell for taxes; the place is easy to keep up with everyone helping; and, we don't get run over by progress –"

He smiled, easy, the same old way. Then his face went slack for a moment: " it's too damn bad that some of the old boys who left Midway quit us. I hope they're doing okay." At lunch Jack, the station manager, called about the old man driving down to Harpers Landing to pick up a misplaced order. We loaded the cold weather gear into the pickup, and headed south. Dad suggested we go by way of the old River Road, so I could have my first look at the Colossus called Kennedy Dam. We took a service road that dropped down and hit old Midway Highway. Dad made some more remarks about the " new frontier." He seemed particularly interested in what I was doing, but, not like he was prying. For a few moments, he did get me to thinking about – what was I doing ?

" From what you say Will, it must be pretty busy up north: oil rigs going up; and that pipeline starting; things really moving! That's what I sort of miss, but then I'd just be a sideliner. That's how it should be – older folks should stand back and let the new guys make it their way. You take this dam: a lot of the power is used for rural schools and hospitals " – he paused and lit up a cigar – " your mom might'a come out better, if that thing we called a hospital in Midway would've been like the new one…."

Upriver, to the left, I scanned the ridges that ran north. About a mile away, a column of white smoke drifted straight up in the cold, still morning air. I knew that meant John's log cabin was still inhabited. We turned downriver, south . Actually, it wasn't a river here, anymore. The water rose up the sides of the ancient gorge, spreading out from the stone bluffs, into a widening V that formed a lake. We followed the shoreline, until the ridge that formed one of the bluffs swung the road up over its back. The old man pulled over. It was a perfect site for the concrete and dirt monster that sprawled out before us across the river. " You want to stop and look her over? We can go right down inside into the turbine rooms. Quite a feeling standin' in the guts of that thing." " No – I guess not – maybe later, dad."

As the old man swung back onto the road, I noticed a gantry crane, with an iron neck like a frozen turkey buzzard, perched on a ledge alongside the sheer, concrete belly. That crane got me started, before I really knew what I was saying: "we had one of those cranes on the oil rig for unloading the barges…" " What's that, Will ? "

"I said, we had one of those cranes on the oil rig – God I hate those things! That's what killed Gene Kirkpatrick my lead man, the guy I wrote you about . The crew was just doing a routine job, off- loading some stuff on the barge – I was almost down there with them except I went to pee. That crane was hovering over the crew on the barge. I walked out. One second the crane was up – next second it was down – folded up like a jackknife on the crew. I stood there frozen while Lynn was running past me, yelling 'Somebody call a chopper!' "

"I scrambled down the cat-walk, and my friend Jack was under the frame. We got him out, and they worked a sheet under his back; the blood was slowly fanning out. They got a blanket, and I put it over him, sat down, and took his hand; it was already cold. I can still hear him groaning: ' my back-Will- my back- I need to turn over-if I can just turn over, I'll be fine.' When the chopper landed, he couldn't feel my hand. He lived, but just barely. It was the only day I was not there with the crew—Karma, I guess?"

Power poles, half buried in snow burms, slipped by to the rhythm of the engine. Rolling through the rising and falling hills, the truck left a wake of fine, powdered snow crystals, glistening in the glow of the sunset in the side view mirror. I let the silence seep in and fill out the perfect moment. We were back at the house by eight. Dad made the fire, and started a pot of coffee, while I unloaded the rig. The coffee aroma warmed the chilly air; a shot of Waller's Deluxe mellowed the entire atmosphere. I rolled the hot, smooth liquid over my tongue, letting its sweet fumes fill my head.

Dad started commenting on his conception of life in Alaska: " it's the last American frontier, Will. You made the right choice. Good people up there, I bet – good folks back in Midway too. You helped each other out through the tough times – bet it's like that in Alaska too." He wasn't getting groggy, like some old-timers with their liquor. He just sipped, smoked his cigar, and studied the darkness through the kitchen window. I watched his reflection in the dark pane, and I know he was watching mine.

He continued: " best part of it is the open-endedness of it – you never know what will happen. Whatever it does , it's yours to handle. Old John says ' you're a short time alive – and a long time dead.' He always played it alone, even with his brother Ben – but that's what this country was all about. A man could decide whether to play alone, or pitch together and whip it. And, by God, the fun was just livin' it whether you whipped it or not, alone or not. Go to her boy; you made the right choice! " And choices suddenly made me think of Fil's choice. I finally decided to ease into it, starting with a story about Alaska.

I proceeded gingerly: " talking about choices reminds me of a choice I make when I go Moose hunting. When you're just walking in the woods in Alaska, you're better off to make some noise, better loud. Why? Because there are big animals, with big claws and teeth, the better to kill you with – Grizzlies. But when you're Moose hunting you need to be silent. And I had a bear charge me because I was being quiet – but lucky for me it was a false charge. He stopped before he hit me, or I had to shoot him. He was less than twenty feet when he swerved, and ran away. I had to sit down. I was being quiet for hunting. So you make a choice to put yourself in jeopardy. "

And I kept going: " When I was working on the Alaska railroad, I made friends with a guy called Jim Klee. He was older than me, and had been around the world several times: he had worked construction from here to back; he drove semi -truck; he had been a lightweight boxer; one time he drove white-lightning, bootleg, across state lines; and he had been in World War II, like you. You taught me about mixed whiskey drinks. He taught me to drink straight whiskey, straight from the bottle.

"We were working on the Alaska Railroad, on a pile-driving crew, on a barge on the water. The 70 foot wood piling was vertical, up in the air, hanging by a cable – and it slipped off the cable and started to fall straight down on us, like an axe! I panicked and chose to jump in the water – and instantly realized my mistake. I had on a hard hat, heavy clothing, big tool belt, and steel- toed boots. I was going down fast. I got the tool belt off, and was working on the heavy clothing, when something hit my hard hat. Spang!

"I knew it wasn't the piling or I'd be dead – I grabbed for it! It started pulling me to the surface, and I bobbed up. There was Jimmy with the pole in his hand, pulling me in. If not for him, I wouldn't be talking to you right now. Well, after the job was over, Jimmy made a choice. He took a contract with M. K., and went over to Vietnam to be a Cat-Skinner. He'd been in a war – he understood jeopardy. Well, day one, they flew him in a chopper to the work-site. He got on the Cat, and it was one he knew, so he started it up. And then he slumped over dead.

"It was a sniper of course; the odds caught up with him. But what I didn't tell you was, in World War II Jim was a sniper. I've thought about this a long time: Karma? I don't know; I just know he's dead from a choice. And it's pretty much the choice Fil made, isn't it dad? "

I hadn't fooled him; he knew where I was going. And finally, he spoke straight out. " Your brother needs to get out of that hell- hole, Will. They don't call it a real war, but it kills just the same. When you spoke out against it, I thought you might be wrong about the country being in it. Now, all I know is it's wrong for Fil to be there; just like I knew it was right for me to be in Europe." He glanced at me without a smile, and his eyes questioning.

"You fought this war here at home until 1970. Maybe you can fight it again by savin' Fil: You lost your friend there; maybe you can retrieve your brother. You made a good choice for your life; maybe you can help him make a good one for his. I'm not sure I know anymore," he said quietly.

"Dad, why is Fil so concerned about your health, in his letters? " He almost grinned. " I've been dropping hints to him about having problems, like I did to you. So, when the Red Cross applies for what they call an ' Emergency Medical Leave' for him, he won't go into shock. Doc McMinn agreed he'd back me up. Red Cross already checked with Doc; it's in the works. I'm going to have to take to my bed and stay there for a while."

He rose, went to the door and looked at the sky, and said "I forgot to get the mail. You can go out now, or wait till morning; night, Will. "

I creaked and crunched my way out to the mailbox. The air was sharp to breathe; the metal door singed my bare fingers; an envelope crackled like old parchment. It was a second installment of Fil's ode from the bewildered (no black border.) Dad was in hibernation, so I left the light on, and finished another Irish coffee while reading the latest epistle:

Chapter 3

Howdy Big Bro

No word from you yet, so I assume you don't need money. If this thing reaches you before 15 March, I will still be on a small, highly classified atoll known as the Pearl of the Pacific – referred to around here as "Devil's Island." So you see, the Army offers an unlimited number of experiences to a young man of my caliber-not 50 caliber. On 15 March I will have an "Emergency Medical Leave", I am assured – which makes me uneasy – to fly home and see Dad. We had both better go home, Will. Has Dad written you about his health? If you make it before I do, we can rendezvous at Seattle Airport on the 15th. Is old John still on his place? Have you heard what they intend to do if he refuses to budge? Hopefully he won't kill anybody – if he does hopefully it will be somebody important.

Your Loyal Centurion, Sir Fil.

I took another sip, and noticed it was 11 at night, and thought of the news. It'd been a very long time since I'd seen the " War at Six and Eleven." I immediately perceived that it looked like continuous reruns. As it faded in, old eyes with young faces stared at the camera as if it might explode. Fingering M-16 rifles, young bodies kept twisting this way and that until I begin to get twitchy. A fallen form lay with head wrapped in battle dressing bandages. Suddenly, I recalled my convalescence at Grammy's house, the summer of '48. Bandaged head propped up on the pillows, I watched for the war raging in the apple orchard, always trying to spot my little brother. Now I knew what face I was searching for on that screen (but they aren't using green apples.) I slammed the off button.

Turning out the light, I crawled into a chilly sleeping bag. My dreams were like bad television programming: Fil, mummified in bandages, wandering through a jungle – Jim Klee with a dog tag from another war sticking between his teeth – John Wester's weathered oak face appearing from under rushing water, his lips repeating a message, but no sound from the agonized mouth. Someone finally hit my off button.

The next week suddenly brought longer days and warmer weather. V's of geese, leaving the river breaks, floated across blue skies into the northern horizon. Kids, at recess on the melting playground, waved to me as I went by. I contacted the Army, and by a miracle, they got a message to Rolly to meet me in Seattle. The old man was not that happy to stay in bed and play sick. But, I could tell how glad he was that Rol was coming home. So, 15 March, I crossed the mountains once more to battle the metropolis.

Winter still held on in Snoqualmie Pass. Lake Ketchlus retained its scurf of rotten ice, over a gray- green surface. Under the ice shield, restless waters forced up long, jagged ridges across the broken ice-field. (Any day now, she'll bust loose and fill the creeks; water will rush down into the streams, and into smaller rivers; and those'll run into the Columbia, and the water will rise… .)

Seattle greeted me with an April shower in March (April showers from October to May – Eastern Washington, across the mountains, is semi-desert-) I found the airport about the same as when I had arrived from Alaska. A line of cabs dozed in front of vacant stalls. I checked for Les Everman's, but they all looked the same. Fil's plane had landed, so I had him paged. He sloshed out of the bar, and enveloped me in a smog of Bourbon. " Hiya big bro! I got a running start on ya . Les' have a drink to welcome me 'ome. "

Fil looked hale and hearty, and with a bit more dubious expression than I remembered. He was still a little taller than me, about 5 foot 10. The Army had done some good; it brought him down to around a trim 160. The GI glasses, however, could not suppress the old, ironic glint in his bloodshot eyes. (He must really be hitting the bottle.) We left Seattle, gladly.

The trip to Newport was a gas. Fil regaled me with tales of the service; it sounded like it hadn't changed much. I told him the stories of working on the oil rigs, and the railroad, and such. Each of us enjoyed the other's experiences, but he kept hitting a bottle he had in his coat. He finished the bottle as we were heading into Cle-elum. When I started talking about Jim Klee, the combination of alcohol, the darkened highway sliding under us, and the isolating hum of the engine, all brought out the feeling that I had never really explained the whole thing before. As I talked, I began to realize things I'd never been aware of about Jimmy Klee.

"Jim looked about 45, but he was actually 58 – he lied to the railroad. But those 58 years sharpened his sense of humor, instead of dulling it, like most people. Wherever there was a buck to be made, Jim tried to make it; most of the time it was just a shade over the legal boundaries. He could make the whole thing sounds like a grand adventure with a humorous twist at the end. It was like the time he told about driving down the Methow Valley, heading for Wenatchee, with a trunk load of his finest white lightning. Western Washington called it "Blue Rain."

"Suddenly, a black Ford came up on him, fast. He said 'I figured it was the feds, so I stomped on it, and so did he. We was flyin' down the grade, and he started layin' on his horn, and me listenin' to my pistons swapping holes. Then my engine cratered, blew a valve, and oil smoke poured out from under the hood, like a rig a' fire. I coasted over to the shoulder, and got ready to jump, and head for the brush.

But when I opened that door, that damn fool nearly ran me over. He went screaming by like a turpentined cat, with a streamer of tin cans and a 'Just Married' sign on the back. And I yelled ' ya, better get to that motel before she closes! ' Then old Jim would laugh, blue eyes sparkling, and take another jolt of straight Waller's Deluxe."

(As the tale of Jim's fate unfolded, I began to see him as a man living in a vacuum.) "Always, when things started going against him, he would cut and run; it looked like his trademark. When he drifted onto the Alaska Railroad, he didn't have a dime – and from what he said, I'm pretty sure legal people were looking for him. He kept reliving his past, over and over, avoiding growth in his future, which ended abruptly when he climbed onto that cat in Nam."

Fil jerked and sat up straight, with his eyes kinda' glazed: " Will, when I get it together, I want to tell you about some of the shit coming down over there." He took another draw on his bottle; " I also lost people and a lot more, in that shit-hole… ." Then he drifted out, and I went on talking.

"Jim musta' given my p.o. box 1766 as his address. They sent me his tools and stuff. And you know what else I got? A notice of his death, and his dog tags, from World War II. Isn't that a kick in the balls? He survived the infantry in Europe 25 years ago. This wasn't his war was it? " I was nearly shouting now. And Fil barely whispered: " whose war is it, Will? " And then he was out cold.

As we got near Newport, Fil sat up and opened his window. The freezing air brought him alive again. So I said, " you can visit with the old man tomorrow. He'll have to stay in bed, to make it look good. But, he and I have been doing some talking. And you and I need to head out somewhere and pow-wow about what's happenin' with you, Fil." In the cool dark, I felt him tighten up: " I know, Will; I read between the lines of the old man's letters. I knew you two had something goin'. You think there's any chance Hoover's boys have tagged you as been' back in the country? "

"I don't know. I pretty well dropped out of sight in Alaska. It would be tough for them to trace me to places like Talkeetna and Nushigek. Hell, they couldn't even locate those places with a roadmap, or their asses, with both hands. " He and I chuckled, and I ended with, " but, I'd feel better if we were out along the river, somewhere." Fil looked up at the dark sky: " they gave me five days and after tomorrow I've got three left." "Okay Fil, let's plan to leave tomorrow afternoon." I felt tired, slightly drunk, and damn good (we're all home again!)

Next morning, the old man played the perfect bed case; he even hammed it up a bit. " But it got me breakfast in bed, didn't it? " He gloated. I know he felt like the rest of us, whole again. He and Fil talked about everything except the war. It was understood that Fil and I would be dealing with what was to be done about that.

Early afternoon, we loaded the rig with camp stuff, and my duffel bag full of rain gear, and sleeping bags. Fil looked more like himself in my ragged jeans, wool shirt and a beat up Stetson the old man offered. We swung through town and picked up grub, and some beer, then headed for the hills. They were turning April pale green at last. Big, yellow grasshoppers whirled toward us, and spun upward as we rushed ahead; some of them kamikazed on the windshield. Here and there, little dust devils swirled themselves into a frenzy, and then vanished, to reappear in another dry wash.

As a road came into view on the right, Fil beat me to the suggestion: " let's stop off and see if old John's around. I could use a piss call. " I swung onto the dirt road (someone had taken down the Midway sign) and we dropped down into what had once been the old riverbed, millions of years ago, when the ice receded. Man was reversing the process, rapidly re-filling the massive glacial cut with water. Stepping out of the pickup, I gazed around at the sweeping sand and stone buttes, rising above the cabin and the river-lake below.

The log cabin looked like something out of the 1800's, and nearly was: wind and sun weathered walls, and roof drooping down, and heat faded windows. " Who the hell are ya, and what you want? " A cracked but, as usual, tough voice called from behind the closed door. "John Wester! It's me, Will Tully, and there's someone else here wants to see you."

An iron bolt rasping back, a door creaking open a crack, and John poked his head out. Eyes squinting in the noonday glare, white hair hanging straight down to his shoulders, with a gaunt, but still standing -straight frame, he put a wavering hand to his forehead, Indian fashion. " Well, don't stand out there in the dust and heat. Hello young Tully, I thought you lit out for the territory for good. I think I recognize the guy with you." He turned and we followed him into the darkness. As I passed through the doorway, I almost stumbled over a long object leaning against the jamb; it was John's ancient 45-70 Winchester rifle.

The place was just as I remembered it. Bed, table, and chairs fashioned from native timber, shiny and seasoned from years of use. The kitchen shelves were plain lumber, ends of old boxes. An ancient coffee pot rested on the back of the smoke blackened, caste- iron range. A musty odor of wood smoke, tobacco, and damp newspaper hung like age in the air. John sat down on a faded army blanket at the foot of the bed, and motioned towards the chairs.

"Sit – you want coffee? The mugs are up there and you can see the pot." He stoked up his pipe and I rolled a smoke. As I struck a match, the sound of water slopping over gravel made me pause. Then I realized that the lakeshore was only a few feet from the back door. " They say you joined the service, that right? " With eyes squinting but still bright, he peered at Fil. " Yeah I'm just doing my duty over in Vietnam, John. " His old eyes narrowed, like an eagle trying to get a better look, as he puffed on the corncob. " I don't hear much about it; but I don't figure it's changed much. Probably like the one I was in, the war to end war, WW I. Hell, my old man did a hitch in the militia, over in Spokane, when the Army tried to drive the Nez Perce Indians onto a reservation in 97."

We sipped our coffee, and let old John go on. "The old man said a lot of guys thought it was great fun, marchin' around, getting drunk, gallopin' horses through the streets. Them injuns was a small bunch that got in the way of progress. They killed some folks who moved on to their land, and that put the Army on them. The way the injuns figured, the whites were invading their land, trying to partition it. They had a treaty and a right to try and stop them. But they were out-numbered, and knew when to withdraw. Then, they all lit out for Canada, called it 'Grandmothers Land' cause' of Queen Victoria in the old days."

John paused, re-lit his pipe, and added, "well, my dad said the defense money was a real boon to the economy. Said the state guv'ment got their cut, the gin mills got their cut, and a few folks at home got the rest. He always used to laugh when he told me that." John's face wrinkled a bit at the corners. He took a sip of coffee, and gazed at Fil. " Wars: all the same—No winners—All losers. " Wind- swept water slopped and grated over gravel behind the back door.

He turned to me, " I figured you was long gone, boy. Don't tell me things was too tough for ya' in the territory. I didn't figure anything was too much for you… ." I gave him a grin: " Nope – I'm just passing through, I guess. I came to see this guy and the old man, and then go back to Alaska. Fil and I are heading up river for a spell, to see how things look, now." John turned his head and looked out the window, toward the lake: " things have changed a bit, real progress they say. Country hasn't changed, just a little wetter is all. The people, they've changed though… ." He rose and reached for a pot on the shelf. " You boys stayin' to dinner, I reckon? "

Fil went to the truck for his bottle, and a few other things. I took John's water bucket and went around to the front of the cabin, down to the shore. On the other side, where the glacier had cut through solid rock, the water rose against sheer, black walls. On John's side, the rising flood was more noticeable. As I dipped the bucket, an object jutting from the water, about 10 feet from shore, caught my eye.

The roof of John's shed stood motionless against the wind driven water. Occasionally, a wave washed across the tarpaper roof, turning it shiny black. But it resisted, returning to its original gray after a few moments in the sun. I scooped up the water, and returned slowly to the cabin. We finished supper, and sat around smoking, and drinking Irish coffee, supplied from Fil's bottle. John loosen up on a full belly, and a drink, and started re-living old times around Midway:

"I tell ya' there was good folks around here, then. If you needed a hand, they didn't wait for you to ask, they just jumped in. No one tried to take what the other guy had worked for. And if you was doing good, fine – if the other fella was doing better, good for him. Shit! I wish I had some of my Blue Rain to offer you boys; I'm out right now." I pictured the submerged shed, outback; " that's okay John, we have to hit it pretty soon, anyhow."

"Don't rush off – but if you boys got places to go, better get on it. Fil finished his coffee and rinsed out the cup with the dipper of water: " Ya', we figured on heading up river, towards Kettle Falls, and camping just this side of the Canadian line." John knocked out his pipe on the side of the bed; dying sparks struck the floor at his feet. " That's a nice trip, good country up that way, good people too. No traffic on the old road, since that new highway cut up to that new town. How's your old man doing up there, Will ? " " The old boy's still kicking around; he seems to like it."

"Yeah – I guess some folks might like it. I didn't care much for the old town, and I can't say I have much use for the new one." He moved back to the bed. " You say you're going up toward the Canadian line? I headed up that way in, let's see, must've been the fall of 18. Yeah, then my brother was down in Yakima working for a rancher. Well, couldn't get any work around here, so I was going to see about gettin' on the Canadian-Pacific Railroad the Canuks was building.

"I was coming down the last draw, and she hit hard, just busted loose with a howler. The snow was so damn thick I couldn't make out the trees. The pony, he couldn't make out things neither so he stopped. I figured we might have a chance if we could find shelter and get a fire going. Then, the wind lulled for a second, and I heard a horse whistling, off to the right. My pony whistled back, like he recognized an old friend. That horse took me right into a ranch yard, and stopped at the corral. I was so damn stiff – it was all I could do to get down – and I stumbled toward the kerosene lights where I figured the house must be.

"And you know," John leaned forward and his gray eyes lost their distant, watery look; " that fella Bunnell, Frank Bunell, he put me up for three days, until the storm blew out, and wouldn't take a dime for it. They was fine folk. I made a little money on the railroad, so I stopped by, on my way back through. And I dropped off some stuff I picked up in Lincoln, real coffee and such. They was so glad to get that stuff, like it was Christmas."

" What the hell does that hombre want? " John's voice went hard, and suspicious. In the yard, a dark green sedan stopped; the driver got out and scanned the area. Obviously a passer-through, confused by the change in the road routes. " That's the same color as the state cars! " John headed for the door, reaching for the rifle. " Wait, it's not marked like a government vehic…." He was out on the porch, fumbling under a tarp covered box when I caught up. Throwing aside the canvas, John grasped a "T" shape handle that rose from a metal box. Wires ran from the box, over the porch rail, and down into the sandy soil.

The car occupants gazed nervously out in wonder at the apparition standing before them. Long white hair shaking wildly, Winchester in one hand, plunger in the other, John called out to the perplexed driver: " I've had it with you state people coming down here and threatening me. You get back in that buggy, and use the whip, or I'll bring the sky down on the whole bunch of us! ! " Needing no further clarification, the driver dove in, larupped the horses under the hood, and vamoosed. John shook the rifle for effect while laughing at the retreating wagon.

John was still chuckling when he said, " I got the whole front yard wired up. One shove on this blaster and nobody will get any benefit out of this place." He covered the box and turned towards me: "suppose you think I've been smokin' Loco-weed. Well, you ain't lived here for the last 80 years." We went in. "

That wind out there isn't getting any calmer, and we have a few miles to cover; so we better hit it, right Will? " Fil rose, stretched, and looked at me. " Yeah, we should head out before she gets too late. Thanks for the coffee and the supper John – take care."

" Well, stop by on your way back if you have time – and howdy your dad for me." John let us out the door. As I turned to climb into the pickup, I got a final look at him: with white hair falling over the shoulders of that faded red and black checkered Mackinaw, and the ragged, frayed Levis, and worn- out boots and slouch hat, he was the image of something I'd seen before, but I couldn't remember where.

Then, he raised his hand in a gesture of farewell, and it all came back to me: I saw, once more, the Alaska natives standing around the taxi strip at the Anchorage airport – faces carved from solid ivory, with old, dark eyes staring out at the new order – comprehending nothing and everything.

Chapter 4

Fanned by steadily rising gusts of wind, shifting flames threw a strange red glare across the black, swirling waters. Fil and I sat brooding over a smoky circle of rocks along the river's edge. Water from the high lakes, streams, and rivers pushed down, down toward the dam, the man made halt in its natural flow where Midway used to be. Through momentary lulls in the wind, I heard surging waters sucking at dirt banks, endlessly trying to reclaim the land it once dominated. Fil suddenly broke into the shifting patterns that I was trying to bring into focus.

"Those clouds heading north, we saw last night, must really be socking it to the high country; there's more water here than I've ever seen, in any year." He stood and gazed upriver, as if to survey the situation, and then weaving down to the river, he faced it and let fly. As he came back up, he observed, " that John, he's the only one I know who can out- yarn the old man. Ya know Will, the best part about those two is, they may stretch things just for the fun of it, but it's all true."

I took a slug from the bottle and closed my eyes: I could see John and the old man, out behind the shop, with the breeze off the river climbing up dune banks and swirling around the poplars. Fil and me, lying on the warm sand, would be listening to stories about the fantastic blizzards in the Dakotas, hauling grain with horses in the winter, laying the great Northern tracks across Montana, the last of the big Sioux tribes leaving the Black Hills – stories John's old man told, long before our dad was even born.

Fil kicked up the fire sending sparks to the wind, then he continued: " you know Will, I remember one time old John was into the story about working the railroad, in Montana. And then he spoke real low, without moving his gaze: ' you know, that railroad? It opened the land for people. But most of em' never had to work a tap to get out to the frontier. They just rolled on out to this country, and started settin' up their stores and towns, and such. They said it was progress.'

"Then John stood up and stretched, and he looked down the river and said ' that's a mighty fine dam those fellows are building ; make things easier for lots of folks – – I'll stick to kerosene. Those boys just going to work down yonder are in for a little thunder shower. Oh well, their ass'll hit the ceiling when the rain hits him in the face – –! ' "

"But then dad said something I'd never heard him say before, sort of gently questioning: ' but that railroad, John, it carried the wheat and the cows to market; and you and a lot of others did all right by that, didn't you? Maybe some folks see this dam the same way, I don't know? It's hard as hell to judge these things isn't it? ' "

I snapped back to the present. Fil rummaged in his pack, brought out another bottle, and broke the seal. " You know Will, I think medical science should look into that 'Blue Rain' of John's. See what it's done for him: he's a living, farting, cursing, raging 100+-year-old testimonial to its power. But the experiments would have to begin at a young age; without a gradual buildup, the mortician could skip the embalming fluid. I've got a few nominees, among our cadre in Nam, as candidates for the experiments on older specimens."

I laughed and got up to do my duty. Away from the campfire, the dark wind seemed colder. Black water slid by and my stream joined it with a sizzle. Pissing in a river at night, while watching clouds roll over the stars, will always be an aesthetic experience for me.

Then I returned, " you know what I was thinking, while John was spinning that yarn about old days in Midway? It sounded to me like he was describing what Alaska is like – the people and all – today. That story about getting lost in a storm reminded me of some things that happened to me up there. I was going from my homestead cabin over to Russ Strauss', and a snowstorm hit I knew I might be in trouble because it would cover my snowshoe tracks, if I tried to go back.

"I figured it was around minus 15 degrees – with wind-chill maybe minus 20. Up ahead, I thought I recognized a clump of Spruce and headed for it. When I got there, I looked around, and suddenly I saw a little flash of light through the storm swirl. Instantly I knew what it was; Russ had hung a lantern from his porch. He said he put up the light because he thought I had said I might come over that day. Russ is the guy who always said: ' in this country you better work with the North wind, or you might not ever work again! ' Russ and Roxie put me up till the storm stopped days later."

I could tell that Fil had been listening, and at the same time, working over something he had on his own mind. The fire spluttered and popped, and a tiny spray of ashes blew up in the wind. We listened to the river sough and sigh. Then he spoke: " it sounds like you've found your life, Will. I hope that dad has re-found his. It was a real jolt for him to leave that fire – insurance man's nightmare he called the shop. You know he was an artist; he could fix anything made of metal with that torch."

I was recalling waking up late at night and watching that torch spread its flickering halo around the dark shop yard. Crickets harmonized with frogs, both competing with the warm, sweeping wind off the river. Odors of cooling sage mingled with an acrid smell of heated metal. The open screen and bleaching pine boards of the summer porch forming a cozy niche, that was how I remembered Midway.

"Dad could resurrect anything made of metal;" Fil entered my reverie. "The summer after you left, John came down from that hermitage of his, and walked into the shop. Dad and I were doing some dental work on the teeth of a sickle cutting bar that bit into a rock. Dad cut the torch and raised his hood. He tapped the weld with his slag hammer, inspected the sickle teeth, then noticed old John. He winked at me and said, ' you're next John. Were having a special today on dentures… make you the finest set of plates ever. They can be hard on the silverware though, if you ain't careful. '

"John just drew on his cigarette and looked us over with those cool, gray eyes. " Then Fil started imitating John's voice: " my stove kinder' went lame. She just sorta sagged over towards one corner, and that damn fool coffee pot decided to dive onto the floor; the coffee tasted bad enough." " We were busting a gut; but you know old John, he wouldn't let on, even if he knew he was being funny. So we loaded up the truck, and headed upriver.

"We fixed the stove and were admiring our work, when John said to sit a spell on the front porch, and disappeared around the corner. He reappeared, carrying three fruit jars of smoky brew; dad sipped his, and stated, 'you haven't lost your touch, John.' I was willing to take his word for it, but John was watching me, so I gave it hell. It went down fine, like cough syrup – then it hit bottom – I knew instant defeat. When I could hear again, John was in the process of pronouncing it the best yet! Dad was looking up at him, grinning."

Fil looked up at a dragonfly that rose sharply over the fire: "I once loved to see those things fly. But, now they remind me of Helio- gunships skimming over rice paddies." I felt like there had been a bit too much whiskey, and stories of the past, to start talking about the future that night. I rolled into a cold sleeping bag under a damp shelter tarp. Fil did the same, humming to himself and stumbling some.

(Fil's leave is up tomorrow, except for travel time!) I realized that, even before coming fully awake to smells of smoke and bacon frying. He was up and cooking, whistling, while dropping eggs into the pan. " Boiled coffee with some dog's hair if you need it," he called. " You must have quite a tolerance built up, if you're drinking that stuff in your morning coffee, Bro." He handed me a plate of salty pork and eggs. "It goes down better than some Gor-mett stuff I've had in fancy restaurants," I noted. He nodded his head, " better than Army chow." " So it hasn't changed since 58, huh? "

After doing the dishes in the river, we put stuff away, and just sat around the fire. " We're near that old pole corral, up on the summer range aren't we," he spoke from under his hat without lifting his head. " Let's hike up to that old cattle roundup area; you can see the river really stretched out up there." I agreed, and we stuffed some snacks in packs, and started toward the hill. I noticed Fil had left his bottle, so I went back and filled one of the empties from the river.

Magpies occasionally floated across our path, landed a ways from us, and then at our approach catapulted themselves on stiff wings down toward the trees. Fil threw rocks at an obsolete sign advertising Orange Rush, available at "Bo Henry's" in Midway. Bo's was now serving the canals of Midway, under the Columbia. I made a halfhearted throw and got a tinny ' clang! ' of stone meeting sign.

A sandy slope, covered with ancient wheel ruts nearly filled in by weeds and wildflowers, announced the road to the old round- up corral. I paused, open the bottle, and let now warmish river water run down my throat. Fil did the same, and we started up 3 miles of heat, rolling hills, and sagebrush.

"I'm thinking about when John used to tell how this place was a hideout for that bandit, Ras Lewis – who operated between here and Cle Elum in the 1920's, " Fil spoke as he sat on the wobbly top rail of a skeleton pole remuda. Its circle was broken by fallen rails and missing posts. " John said he and the Sheriff once trailed Lewis to here, but Ras got word they were commin' and lit out." I opined: " I'da hated to have old John trailin' me, when he was in his prime. He was still a damn good shot with that 45 – 70 Buffalo rifle when I was in school.

"I don't know if you remember, Fil, how John told about what happened in CleElum? He said an old man showed up there, in about the 30's, and it got around that he might be Butch Cassidy, out of Bolivia. Now this was about the time that Ras Lewis disappeared, and eventually some people started putting things together. Lewis and Cassidy were both wanted by the law. But some folks thought Lewis wanted to hide behind somebody big time. When the sheriff started asking around, Lewis – Cassidy both disappeared. They think he went to Canada."

He jumped down and wandered toward the remains of a log and sod cabin. Burned into the wood rails, cattle brands lay like symbols from a prehistoric tribe. I ran my finger around the deep grooves, and felt the Circle T in the wood. The place was a real Western American relic.

"This all reminds me of Les Everman's place when they packed up and left that day " Fil nodded down toward the ghost corral. We sat down on a fragment of stone foundation; the warm rocks felt good on my butt. He continued, "you weren't there when that happened. Les was workin' on the dam, and he got pissed at a foreman. The guy had a reputation for spoutin' off about the farmers gettin' paid more than a fair price for their land, because of the dam."

He took out some cheese, I got out the rolls, and we ate in the shade of the cabin wall. Clouds were rolling up from the south, on a wind that swayed the sage and rustled loose boards. Fil went on,

"Les kicked the shit out of that foreman, jumped in his pickup, and headed for home. He went by our place like a maniac. I figured there must be an emergency, so I followed him in dad's rig. He was so damn mad, he drove through – I mean right through – his own gate bars When I got there, he was throwing stuff around and yelling 'pack up, Shirley, we're gone. We ain't spendin' another night here! '

"Then, he went to the barn and started hauling out a bunch of stuff. I walked inside the stables and looked around: dead straw, dried manure, and dust oders rose out of the cool dirt floor. He went by me several times, and then I asked what he was gonna do with all that stuff. He just stood there with an old iron hay hook in his hand.

"He looked at the hook, then at the pile, then at the walls: he swang that hook in a wide arc over his head, and he sank it at least 2 inches into one of those peeled tree posts. It sounded like an axe hitting old oak- Thonk ! He shoved his hands into his overall pockets, and stared out the doorway: ' FUCK IT ! Let it all go with the place!' " Fil finished: " we walked past the heap, and out through the pole corral." "I didn't tell you, but I saw Les in Seattle, Fil ; he didn't look or sound that good." We finished the meal quietly, just letting the wind and the sun play across our silent, shared memories. Coming back, we both stopped on a ridge and loosened our shirts to let the wind blow across our sweating bodies. It left a rime of salt and grime, but it felt really fine (poetry?)

Back at the truck, great black clouds, ominously bulging with rain, like WW II Navy spotter blimps, coasted across the sun. I was awed by the storm front piling up against the mountains. " Those guys down at the dam are in for it, uh Will. Oh well, I guess their ass'll hit the ceiling, when the rain hits 'em in the face. " We both grinned. Eating silently, we sat enveloped in smoke and apprehension. (How to say what needs to be said, and have it come out right?)

"Hey Bro, do you think maybe Les Everman and John are applying the wrong solution to a problem that we all refuse to face? The way I see it, the problem is knowing when to fight, and when to run. Know what I mean? " " I know just what you mean, Will. The whole damn country. . ." Giving dramatic punctuation to Fil's comments, the northern skies rumbled eerily. We both looked up the river, then at each other, and into the fire.

"Sounds like the airstrikes on nights when Charlie gets too close," he mused. I watched yellowish flames creep along a stick, flaring and shrinking with the breezes. I went on: " Les, the old man, John, all of them lost something; I know how that feels. But the real hell is, not knowing why. I know that too." Fil was sitting with his eyes closed, listening to me and to himself.

"It's like the day Joe stumbled into our apartment at Washington U., and puked out the horror of Kent State. I'm still not sure why that happened; but I have an idea how it happened." I motioned for him to pass the bottle. The warmth flowed in; the breath rushed out.

I continued: " I once met a guy named Bruce working at a crab cannery at Kodiak. We got to know each other, and finally swapped stories of how we came to Alaska. It's something everyone up there does. It was the damnedest thing bro. We were on opposite sides of the barricades, but Kent put us both on the run. Bruce was in the Kent R. O. T. C. when it happened. He told me he'd more or less planned on going   ' over there ' after graduation.

"He said he hadn't known any of the demonstrators, personally. It did piss him off that they trashed the 'ROTC Y' building." Fil's bottle became more active as my story unfolded. " The way Bruce explained it, he just felt like some junior military observer – until the guns went off. He never thought the government would actually kill its own youth, kids like himself. He said ' that's when I instantly understood that kids, American or Asian, were real kids – real dead kids !! ' "

"Bruce burned his uniform, stuffed his clothes in a pack, and headed for the freeway entrance. You know what he had written on the inside of his pack flap when I met him? It said: ' Bloody Kent will never die as long as we try to speak the truth in this country! ' He really lost something, bro, and he's still trying to figur' out why. "   I watched Fil go into a slow roll beside the fire, flames glinting off the bottle in his hand.

Putting the bottle to his mouth, Fil laid down, all in one motion. He looked like a modernesque sculpture of a water cooler. Then, using the empty bottle as it kinescope, he peered up through it at the gathering storm. " I found the answer, Will ; the answer's at the bottom of the bottle! " He continued on: " I'm putting together a movie; you want to see some scenarios? I view them through my magic lens, here." Squinting into the bottleneck, he turned an imaginary crank and provided the soundtrack .

[Thanks to Al Scott for some of the following Viet Nahm scenes.]

"Opening scene is an aerial shot of a blood- red dawn coming 'up like thunder across the China Sea.' The shadowy silhouette of a Buddhist Sham Temple emerges from the jungle hillside. Next, we cut to the temple courtyard as it gets lighter, and tiny sparrows begin twittering in the bamboo trees. All this wrapped in barbed wire and signs in English and Vietnamese saying 'Mine Secured Area.' And, in the dawn's early light, we see huge, ear -like antennas rising from tiled roofs."

Fil's college courses in Cinema were evident. A cold gust sweeping up the dunes made both the fire and me quiver. The grotesque war movie ground on... . "Cut to an interior shot of the temple's main prayer area, filled with communications equipment – huge radio transmitters – encoding machines- decoding machines – a technician's dream. And, day and night – above the crackle of distant voices calling from remote jungle hideouts – always the constant whirring of chopper wings coming and going, shuttling secrets to and fro." His voice dropped to a stage whisper – " secret, secret, I've got a secret! "

I let him go. It had to come out, and the inner fire was glowing through him. He burned on. . . " How you like it so far folks? Cartoon time; remember the old double features? Pathos then Bathos. In the background, we see the remains of a big party with a punch bowl on the table. Standing on the table is a 'Vietnamese girlfriend' washing her pussy in the punch bowl.

"Cut to the exterior of a 'skivvy shack' in a drab little village, in a drab little country, in a drab little South East Asia. Two olive drab G. I.'s are leaning against the stair rail. We hear their drab little patois: ' I told you he wouldn't know what to do – he's been in there for damn near an hour, Jack.' Re Jack: ' I don't care if he has to make installment payments – he needs this and I'm glad we did it! Remember how he sat there and told us about never getting laid, how he could never talk to girls, how he felt they didn't like him? He must be 35, and has hardly even talked to a woman. '

"'Well he must be just talking to her, Jack. We really had to pour it down him to get him to come here; maybe he passed out?' 'Ahh give me a jolt of that shit and – wait, I hear someone coming –' both guffaw at the pun. Cut to the doorway of the hooch. There appears a figure in drab civilian clothes, the kind that look like Army issue. He wears a beatific, bleary expression. As the camera pans downward, we see his weary manhood still dangling out of his open fly. They Were Triumphant! " Fil shouted the last words.

"They gave Sgt. K. an ' L. B. J.' – you know Lyndon Bains Johnson-- Lousy Blow Job – that's what we called a hand job. He never knew what it was all about." Fil prepared to roll the camera again by opening another bottle. I shifted near the feeling of security from the fire, and lowered my head. It felt like the first two scenes were just illumination flares, sent up to light the area; the real battle was just starting.

"Fade in on the semi-lit interior of the Buddhist temple. A young G. I. sits hunched over a decoding machine, his form tense, eyes darting back and forth over the printed readout : Intel about the Big Bang at DaNang : Explosions still occasionally jolt the area; the rockets red glare still light up the night ; intense smoke is clearing; and the search teams scour the perimeter. No official explanation yet as to the devastation of Ammunition Supply Point, I Core Area. Unofficial estimates of casualties are very light.

"The camera closes in on a tight shot of the machine print out, written in ' military speak.' As it passes through the G. I.'s hands, he reads the words that appear from the bowels of the decoding monster :

"cryptographic Code ordinance destruct. at Zulu
sector deter. to be V. C. Sapper teams led by N. V.

A. Advisors – total loss of Ord. Confirmed – Our Body Count undeter. – Assumed to be near total loss of personnel, incinerated due to giant heat blast – Anti- personnel gas released by explo. counts for more – poss. total loss est. at near 500+ – A C8 2 H B – X X X."

"The choppers come and the choppers go, but the bull shit goes on forever ! The End!! None of that will go out to the American public, Will. Even when they know the grapevine will spread the truth up and down Vietnam. I guess they figure the old vine won't stretch across the Pacific ocean. Sure, it's a war ; sure there has to be secrets. But I work with secrets every day – and I can't tell anymore what's real ! They're even lying to themselves, Will, and they don't even know it." Mechanically, he tipped up the bottle and guzzled.

Chapter 5

With the wind rising, we caught small flashes of lighting up-country. I finally realized that I needed this meeting as much as Fil. "Maybe there's been war for so long (a million years ?) that nobody on the planet knows what's real, Bro. Maybe we need a president with a sign on his desk – ' the fuckin' bull shit stops here! ' But how would we know; how would he know? "

"listen Will, a guy in H. Q. sold insurance in L. A. He said the company always screwed people, and I asked him once how they could get away with it. He said, ' Just so it doesn't happen with too many people, all at once, were O. K. We play the averages; and we always win, don't we ? '

"And the people over there are getting horribly screwed, sometimes literally Will !! – A guy went to Saigon for RnR, hit a bar, and picked up a ' girl friend.' She took him home, and he screwed her, and paid her. Then a baby started crying, and he suddenly realized it was Christmas Eve. He said, ' it's Christmas; there has to be something for the baby!' Having no money left, he gave her his cigarette lighter, ' for the baby. ' " (and It has only happened a billion times in the history of war.)   " And Thailand is one big whore house for American forces, Will !"

Then in a quiet-scary voice he said— " This is going around the bars over there: to end the war, put all the friendly 'gooks ' on ships; nuclear bomb the country flat; sink all the ships. They call it ' the Final Solution ! ' " (Only use atomic bombs when you can't win any other way.)

"What do you suppose would happen if we tried to get T. V. air time to call together all the mothers, fathers, wives, and children of all the guys that damn jungle has swallowed up. We would ask them, each one, what their loved one died for! I can't tell you what the hell I may be dying for – can you? "

He was up, waving his arms around, yelling, nearly falling in the fire. The flames gave his eyes a spooky glare. I grabbed him and held on, but I couldn't answer his question. (Final body count 50,000 dead. But what about all the grunts with invisible wounds carried with them forever, and Fil, and me, and all the Joes ? No one will ever really know. And then there's the 1 million Vietnamese vanished.)

I finally lowered him gently against a log by the fire, and threw his parka over him. I suddenly felt cold water, growing into a drizzle, that had been falling for a while. Semi- conscious, Fil called out: " I'll title it: ' A Farewell to Arms and Legs, and Heads and Souls.' They'll just add it to the W W II reruns on the late show, ha? " He started to speak again – suddenly, a glare shot out of the brush behind us, and spread over the churning water. We jumped up and whirled around into the twin beams of pickup headlights. An excited voice carried above the roar of the wind and water.

"I seen your campfire – better pack up and head for high ground – man on the radio says water's building up fast this side of Grand Coulee – gonna' be a real gully washer! " A door slammed, gears ground into reverse, and the headlights jerked away at a right angle; then, wet red taillights glistened rapidly into the distance.

Even in his condition, Fil's war reflexes rapidly crammed bedrolls and stuff into his pack. Sputters of steam rose from the dampening ashes, as I sweated and crammed gear into my duffel bag. My hands struck something in the dark of the bag. Pots and pans jangled against those damn dog tags. I almost pitched them over my shoulder into the river, but then shoved them into my pocket. We threw the gear into the bed, and climbed into the chilly, damp cab; he dug into the glove box for the keys.

The motor caught, and I shoved it into low; we spun out of the river gravel and onto greasy, dirt tracks. At the pavement, I paused, and he looked around. " We can make it north to River City, and head up to the new highway from there." I nodded, " yeah, that's probably the shortest route to high ground ."   I cranked the wheel to the right, and started to release the clutch – "old John! – He doesn't have a radio, and he might not get the word !. It's 20 miles to his place." I felt queasy just saying it.

Fil looked at me then quickly glanced ahead into the glare of falling water: " we must have a little time, who knows how much? We could pick John up, and then it's just a hop to the Newport cut- off." I wheeled the pickup into the southbound lane, and ran the whining engine up thru the gears. Tires gurred wetly; wipers beat against the hood. Gail winds blew sheets of spray across the tunnel made by the **high beams. We both concentrated on the shiny pavement rolling underneath us. Just beyond the reach of the headlights, two wide, yellow eyes flared; a form glided across the road, and down into the ditch, as we whipped by.**

Fil picked up where he left off down by the river. But he was clear and cool under pressure: " I can't help thinking about the comparison you made between John's experiences and yours, in Alaska," he said tightly. " The thing that strikes me is how you two are similar, in a number of ways. But there is a crucial difference…" He handed me a smoke he had rolled; a match filled the cab with a momentary flash. " But," he continued, " whether that difference remains, or whether you become identical to old John is yet to be seen, as I see it. "

"I think you have something you're trying to tell me bro; and I think you're not sure yourself, what it is. But, go ahead and we'll see how it works out, " I replied. Fil shifted around, and, still staring at the road, he spoke carefully: "

you and John are both living on the frontier. I think you see yourself as a new frontiersman – an Alaskan – and there's nothing wrong with that.

"But, basically, your frontier is real; you are living it, now. John's still living on the frontier of 80 years ago, and it isn't working. I've been thinking about this thing the whole time I was in Nahm – and believe me, I put a lot of thought into how I ended up in that nightmare." He reached over and turned on the heater blower.

"When you ran in'70, Will, I thought – ' that's the answer to the problem of my hometown disappearing under water. Be like Will and Les Everman, cut and run –' So I joined the Army and went on the Great Adventure. I know, you told me what the Army was like. But I had to learn for myself. Besides, you'd never been to a war; you just came close in '58.

"Then I started getting dad's letters; those did me more good than anything else. I finally saw that he wasn't going to just chuck it and drift, or fight the flood like John and maybe die. Dad really knows how to roll with it and come up swimming – sorry. " What Fil was saying made more sense, as he went on. It began to bring into focus some of the chaotic images I was fighting in my dreams. As water- soaked highway reeled out before the blurred headlights, I absorbed everything he was saying.

Fil sighed, " so, here we are risking our asses for a guy – a great, old guy – but still a hard-nosed old fart who may get us all killed, just to prove that his dreams are more real than reality. Because you know John won't leave that place easy. " He sank back in his seat; "shit, at least when you saw that guy Gene on the railroad get his with the loading crane, you had the sense to quit a funky outfit. But, you couldn't see the

lesson that Jim Klee's life, and death, could have taught you. So you just cut and ran, again, when Joe needed you. What worries me is that you have the potential to start re-living the same experiences, like Jim Klee did, over and over. And then build them into something that you start thinking is real, but it's not, like John."

I recognized the sharp bend in the road that signaled John's turnoff. Shifting down to second, I brought the truck into rapid deceleration while forming a reply to Fil's speculations. " You may have something here, little brother, but damned if I understand everything I know about it all…." Below us, a pulsing red glow filtered across the ridge in front of the cabin. We broke over the rise, and in the gloom below, a flashing beacon of a State Patrol car swept the wet, black hills, and swollen river that was eating at the cabin.

I eased down the muddy grade, waiting to be engulfed instantly in a wall of water. The bloody , red strobe light effect on cabin and wind-lashed water didn't help my nerves. Then, I saw a State Trooper kneeling by the front fender of the squad car. He was motioning me to hold it. I cut the motor and headlights, and in the semi- gloom raindrops pounded on the metal roof.

Fil started to open his door – a flash of yellow and a roar leapt out of the cabin window ! He dove for the ground, in good rifleman form, and scuttled toward the police car. As I slid out my door, and scrunched down, the thought struck me: (what if Fil is killed here, on home soil, after he got out of that quagmire? Too grotesque even for me to think of.)   I think it hadn't registered with me that we were under fire from old John.

When I moved around the back of the pick up and down the side of the patrol car, Fil and the trooper were already discussing the situation. Re the trooper: " that old bastard is crazier than a coot; he damn near winged Curly! – What the hell is going on – you know anything about it? " Fil offered, " more than I want to." I think Fil suddenly remembered what I had wanted to forget, all along. " That guy in there has been here since before my father, or yours, was born. I love him; but we can't let him get out on the porch. He has this whole yard mined, and the plunger is under that tarp. We may be literally sitting on a powder keg, even as we speak."

Trooper Dan's eyes looked like a man in snake country, as he surveyed the ground under his feet. "That does it! Curly, keep that crazoid in there if you have to shoot him ! I'm calling for backup. Maybe this whole bug-fuckin' place will be downriver before we have to do anything, anyway! " He went for the radio, while Fil and I stared at the porch. In my mind's eye, I could see the patrol cars careening down the grade, red lights bouncing off everything, and John firing a welcoming volley. Suddenly, Curly fired a shot in the air, and John got pinned down before he could get to the Doomsday device. I was glad, and mad and sad.

In our childhood, Fil had always relied on me to produce the strategy. He was a good soldier, maybe too good. But now, he had the real combat experience. I looked at him, and he gave me a sad grin and shrugged: " in Nahm , they'd just call in the air support and level the place. I don't have any ingenious ideas. But we have to at least try to do something. " Trooper Dan returned, shaking his head: "those ass holes can't understand what's going on down here." He turned to Fil: " you say you have an idea of what this guy wants? "

"I think I do, but this isn't the time, or place, to go into details. " He sounded pretty steady for a guy under fire; he must've learned something. Dan spoke, " if he doesn't come around pretty soon, I'm going to let him stay here . I'll be damned if I'm going to drown or get blown up on account of some old geek! " The trooper glanced over his hood, and then back at us. The wind howled and lulled. The radio crackled and a voice issued from the squad car: " Unit 19 – please give update on your situation."

I closed my eyes and pictured the scene from a distance: absurd no matter how you saw it. Then I thought maybe my watching W W II movies at the Midway theater every Saturday might help. I told Fil to stay up by the front fender of the car, and start talking to John: " keep him suspicious so he leaves the barrel of that cannon out the hole in the window."

Fil moved into position: " John, John Wester, it's me Fil Tully. What the hell are you shooting at old friends for, John? " The water-filled air smothered his voice, and he shouted louder: " John, it's me Fil, and Will's here too ! " I crawled around the car, watching the window so intently that I crawled up on something soft, before I could stop. " Whaaaaaaaaat the hell …? " The second trooper yelled and thrashed around, waving his pistol.

Wham! The old 45-70 barked, and a bullet cut the air over our heads. (The Infiltration course didn't really prepare me for the feeling of lead fired in anger.) While Curly and I beat feet for the car, old John's voice rose over the wind: " you bastards figger' there's enough of you out there to take a near 100-year-old man ? Why don't you just get the hell out of here, and leave me alone? That's all I ever asked for! " That's when I knew how it would have to be.

If John was living in the past, he would follow the old rules: you never shoot an unarmed, innocent man who just wants to talk. I stood up and told Fil to follow me: " he's still shooting over our heads; it'll be okay ." The brothers Tully started doing the two-step toward whatever was going to happen.

Chapter 6

"John ! It's me Will Tully; Fil and me are here to talk ; we're commin' in ! " I knew we were safe from his bullets, but only God knew about the water. " Will, you boys better head on out; those cops were trying to tell me somethin' about a flood. Best for you to leave, just in case they weren't bulling me." " We aren't leaving til we talk to you, John – it's up to you! " Gusts of wind blew cold water from behind the cabin.

"Ok, come on in, and say what you have to. Just you boys ! " John squinted through the window, the red glow flitting across his shoe-leather face. " Stop ! " I stood beside the door, leaning against the frame. A steady tattoo of waves in back, beating against the house, reverberated through the jam. John opened the door part way. Fil spoke softly: " tell him Will; tell him it's all over ."

John looked at him, and his gray eyes held a momentary anger. " So it's all over, huh? What do you know about it? What do you know about 90 plus years of living in this country? " I rolled a smoke, slowly, giving myself time to answer John's question, if there was an answer… . " I think Fil means that maybe it's time, John; it's time to change. He means like that story your dad told about the Nez Perce Indians. The whites were invading their land, and they knew they had a right to defend the land according to the Treaty. But they also knew they couldn't defeat the Army. So they started in on the longest, most successful military retreat in American history. And they almost made Grandmother's Land, Canada…"

John's shoulders drooped as he walked to the bed and sat down. " You boys better skedaddle now, I'm getting sort of tired." " We aren't going without you John, so it looks like we all stay," I said. He looked at Fil who took a chair and started rolling a cigarette. I suddenly felt the dampness as a water-filled gust drove in through the back window. I could barely see him loading his pipe, and then flame spurted from his hands. The light played over the black iron stove, reflected in the dark windows around the cabin, and across his ancient face. Waves pounded at the back walls.

"I reckon we better get going – gettin' mighty boggy in this place, " John said as he rose and started clearing a shelf. He was placing a few objects on an army blanket on the bed. Last, he reached for the 45-70 and levered the shells out; they clattered wetly onto the flooded floor. He rolled the rifle into a bedroll with the blanket, then walked toward the door without looking back.

Fil and I started to file out, and waved to the troopers sitting in their car. Then John stood the rifle up against the doorframe, and turned, " I forgot my Pappy's hoss-pistol. He used it in the wa r between the states. I was born 15 years after the war ended.

I paused on the steps. Suddenly, John yelled out from the dark interior – " I been alive for every war we ever fought from 75' on: startin' with Little Big Horn, including Mexicans and Cubans, Kaisers, Nazis, Japs, Koreans, and Commies. I even fought some of them myself! And we never lost, cause' we never give up! And – dammit – I ain't given up!! " He slammed the door like doom !!

An excited dispatcher's voice began crackling over the police radio – instantly, the squad car raced backwards, spun around, tires throwing gravel, and tore up the hill, it's rollers flashing an insane S.O. S. " I've got a terrible feeling they know something we don't ! " Fil lurched around and looked back at the house.

"Run !!" We clawed our way up the oozing sand and gravel bank that felt like the survival climb at Fort Ord, only for real ! As we crawled over the top of the bank, a noise like a giant outgoing tide sucked all other sound out of the wet-black air. I looked down to see a roiling jumble of water, logs, and cabin roof madly swirling away from the shore. Fil lay on his belly, looking over the cut bank, dog tags hanging from a chain around his dripping neck; the gray metal discs clinked on gravel. Over the roiling water and wind, Fil yelled – " I don't need these fucking things anymore! "

He jumped up and broke the chain, whirled it around, and the tags sailed into the roaring abyss. He watched my face. I paused, then drew the hand grenade ring out of my pocket. Rocking back, I pitched my tags, the last remnant of my, and Jim Klee's, military glory. (The Big Eskimo would've been proud of my form.) We moved far up the bank, and sat down, dazed and shaking. " I don't think I'm headed West again, Will. I think I'm headed North, but not as far as you . " " I don't think I'm headed North, just yet, bro."

Mentioning the West reminded Fil of John: "Do you think it might have ended different, Will ? " I replied, " I was standing there thinking, maybe the best end would be if we just left and let Fate decide. I feel like it did, anyway. That's why it's called Fate. I'm going to miss that hard old man!" He looked away. " Yeah, me too, Wil ; he was a major part of our growing up. But I'll tell you what – I got a final lesson from John. Talking about the Nez Perce Indians gave me a clue. The government really wanted to wipe them out, so Chief Joseph headed for Canada. "

"Yeah bro, John's refusal to leave showed us what not to do; his Indian stories showed us what to do: live to fight another day . That's what Joe did ; and I'm going to go find him." " I think you're right Will, another country is better. Besides, Vancouver 's just 100 miles or so from here; I could keep in touch with dad. I ain't given up on this country, but I can do more for it alive. I think the people running it, and the regular people, need a sign, Will. Is that what you and Joe were trying to show? "

"Yeah – we tried given' the gummit a signal, but they just poured boiling oil on the peasants. I guess they never saw the part where our torches ignite the oil and burn up the monster and his master in their own castle. But, I guess I must like the taste of boiling oil, wonder if it comes in flavors? I imagine I can find Joe again, just look for the burning castles."

Fil looked solemn: "do you think Joe might be into something like that Weatherman shit, bombings and stuff ? " " Not unless he's chucked every principle he ever held, man. He's not a hater. Most haters are just people who haven't figured out the lie – the Big Lie – the one that says there is always a 'Us and Them' between the common people of all countries. That's what dictators count on." " Right on Will ! Give em' hell ! "

Rol turned and started for the highway: " I wonder if dad's truck insurance covers flood? If it doesn't, we better both head for Grandmother's Land." Mentioning grandmother suddenly gave me a flash of Grammy's childhood haven from the storms of war. "Hey Bro, you remember that time at Grammy's farm in 48', when we were playing war with Nazis ? And remember how I fell out of that tree and hit the rock; boy were you guys impressed with the blood ; and I got a medal for my only visible war scar. Remember the battles, and how Teddy and I rolled that giant mud ball, the atomic weapon to end all wars, and we annihilated Kirk with it? At least I stopped that war! Not that I'm recommending that way of ending war! Hey, wait up Kilroy!"

A Postscript: Will Tully at 80—My final words-I promise

My memoirs are a record of the life and times of the cold war walking wounded—world-wide we number in the billions. In the book " Walden " H.D. Thoreau wrote that his neighbors led lives of "quiet desperation." Here's my answer telegram:

Dear Henry,

Consider yourself lucky- Stop- My worldwide neighbors' desperation is not only NOT quiet- Stop-

Every day it borders on lethal-Stop- I wish all of them would read your book, and take it to heart,

AND JUST STOP! STOP! STOP! STOP! STOP! STOP! STOP! STOP! STOP! STOP! STOP! STOP! STOP!!!

When you fuck with the forces of Nature-- Nature is the House-- the House always wins. Witness dams breaking— floods—droughts--tides washing over villages—Ice caps melting—massive forest fires—the Pacific with a plastic pollution patch twice the size of Texas--global climate changing— CHERNOBLE –FUKASHIMA –Not fucking-up things in the first place works better than remediation—counting on sticking your finger in the dike is like wearing the condom on your balls.

Here's the bottom line: (thank God)

The other day, I saw a magazine title that pronounced the Cold War as over. My answer: As long as those missiles sit hideously silent in those silos, the Cold War is not over ! The people have simply swallowed this premise: The Nukes are an unalterable fact—like Nature. What they are choking on is this: Man has never invented a weapon that he has not used !- HIROSHIMA-NAGASAKI! The new sign over the gates of

Auschwitz reads: " THIS MUST NEVER HAPPEN AGAIN!! " And (you knew it would come) the real purpose of Nukes has become Crowd Control. The Powers That Be are scaring their own Masses into silence with the threat of The Big One.

If Ford can pardon Nixon—and Trump a bunch of convicted Felons—then Fil can be exonerated !

Let this little tome stand as a memorial to all the unknown, non-soldiers who fought the Nukes and wars in every Middlesex, village, and farm across the nation, and the world. Men and women who gave up families, careers, went to jail—like the Berrigan brothers—and some gave their lives ! And some are still giving their all to stop the insanity of the military's phrase for the policy of countries countering each other with nuclear weapons: Mutual Assured Destruction—aptly called: MAD. WE MUST STOP FORGETTING THAT THE NUKES COULD END CIVILIZATION !!

Will Tully, 2022